DEATH (

A great beaked ꜱ   liar
shape against the   ꞓred
sharphy and swept by us, ...   ꞓard
any other craft make. Joe screamed and backed oars frantically,
and the boat walled out of the way just in time; for though the
prow had missed us, still otherwise we had died. For from the
sides of the ship stood long oars, bank upon bank which swept
her along. Though I had never seen such a craft, I knew her for a
galley. But what was she doing upon our coasts? They said, the
far-farers, that such ships were still in use among the heathens of
Barbary; but it was many along, heaving mile to Barbary, and
even so she did not resemble the ships described by those who
had sailed far.

We started in pursuit, and this was strange, for though the
waters broke about her prow, and she seemed fairly to fly
through the waves, yet she was making little speed, and it was no
time before we caught up with her. Making our painter fast to a
chain far back beyond the reach of the swishing oars, we hailed
those on deck. But there came no answer, and at last, conquering our fears, we clambered up the chain and found ourselves upon the strangest deck man has trod for many a long,
roaring century.

"This is no Barbary rover!" muttered Joe fearsomely. "Look,
how old it seems! Almost ready to fall to pieces. Why, 'tis fairly
rotten!"

There was no one on deck, no one at the long sweep with
which the craft was steered. We stole to the hold and looked
down the stair. Then and there, if ever men were on the verge of
insanity, it was we. For there were rowers there, it is true; they sat
upon the rowers' benches and drove the creaking oars through
the gray waters. *And they that rowed were skeletons!*

SHADOW KINGDOMS

The Weird Works of Robert E. Howard, Volume 1

ROBERT E. HOWARD

EDITED BY

PAUL HERMAN

INTRODUCTION BY

MARK FINN

WILDSIDE PRESS

SHADOW KINGDOMS

Published by:
www.wildsidepress.com

FIRST PAPERBACK EDITION: 2005

Printed in Canada

CONTENTS

TWO-GUN MUSKETEER: ROBERT E. HOWARD'S *WEIRD TALES*

The history of *Weird Tales* magazine is written not by the editors, but by the authors who appeared in its pages. Of all the celebrated authors that have seen print in "The Unique Magazine" ". . . That Refuses to Die," the most influential and important writers to call *Weird Tales* their literary home were the "Three Musketeers:" H.P. Lovecraft, Clark Ashton Smith, and Robert E. Howard.

The youngest of the trio, and also the last one to break into *Weird Tales*, Howard brought his own strengths to the magazine's pool of talent. Smith was already gaining popularity as a poet of some renown. Lovecraft's work, even prior to "The Call of Cthulhu," wasn't like anything else being done at the time; imaginative and thought provoking.

Howard was full of clever and interesting ideas, and he was himself an accomplished poet; it would be easy to say that he was a kind of amalgamation of the two authors. However, Howard turned those traits on the axis of something that would become a trademark of his writing: his flair for action. No one could write stirring, visceral action like Howard, whether it was two men fighting a duel of honor or rival armies clashing for glory. His deftly penned prose and poetry made him one of the most popular writers in the magazine.

And it's no wonder, considering that Howard created his most famous characters and brought them to life for the *Weird Tales* audience: Solomon Kane, King Kull, Bran Mak Morn, and later, the most famous of them all, Conan the Cimmerian. Howard invented the sword and sorcery tale as we define it with his genre-breaking Solomon Kane, and he continued to refine his idea of a good story — fast action, supernatural goings-on, and compelling characters to hang his plots on — with each new manuscript, each new series.

"You gave me my start in the racket by buying my first story — 'Spear and Fang,'" wrote Howard to editor Farnsworth Wright in 1931. "I was eighteen years old at the time." He sold the story to Wright in 1924, but it didn't see print until the following year. Howard kept trying to write for other markets, but no one was willing to take a chance on the young, unknown writer from Texas. Wright, however, kept buying Howard's work, and wrote encouraging things to him. Soon, Howard had three stories scheduled to appear in the magazine — but no money to show for it, as *Weird Tales* paid on publication, not acceptance.

Howard grudgingly returned to college in nearby Brownwood, seeking a diploma in bookkeeping. While at Howard Payne University, he cranked out several humorous sketches for the college newspaper, *The Yellow Jacket*. He also wrote numerous poems and the occasional story, many of which were submitted to *Weird Tales* and other pulps. During the time Howard attended college, his stories and poems were finally appearing in print. Encouraged, he started working on the stories that would later catapult him to the top of Wright's stable of writers — stories of Solomon Kane and King Kull.

With the publication of "Red Shadows" in 1928, Howard became a literary force to be reckoned with. Who was this Solomon Kane, anyway? A sword-wielding Puritan, fighting pirates and witch doctors in the 17th century? Such a story had never been done before. Horror stories were cheap and plentiful in *Weird Tales*. Wright reprinted classics from the likes of Poe, in addition to buying new stories from authors writing contemporary horrors. And the historical adventure was certainly nothing new, either. The historical romance was alive and well in the 1920's, both in classic literature and more modern fare, and even at the movies.

Howard invented sword and sorcery (or if you prefer, heroic fantasy) by combining the two genres. It seems simple and elementary now, but at the time, Howard was stepping out into uncharted territory by taking his love of history (a love shared by Farnsworth Wright) and sprinkling in strange and unexplained events with the intent of having them directly engage the characters. The results were dynamite. Howard had a hit on his hands.

As well liked as the stories were, Wright didn't publish all of the Solomon Kane yarns that Howard sent him. A capricious editor, he rejected Howard's offerings as often as he accepted them. Rather than be discouraged by this, Howard took it in stride and reworked the stories and submitted to different pulps. If they came back again, Howard simply changed tactics and wrote about new characters.

Taking the sword and sorcery concept one step further, Howard then created King Kull in the story, "The Shadow Kingdom." This time, he completely removed any semblance of the world we know and set the tales so far in the past that Atlantis was alive and kicking (and a tribal, barbaric continent, to boot). Kull is himself an Atlantean, and a usurper of the throne of Valusia. With a detailed, if fictitious setting and a strong, savage character, Howard crafted several stories of court intrigue, wizardry, and breathtaking action. Even fewer Kull stories were printed in *Weird Tales*, but they are a vital link to the Conan stories that followed.

Weird Tales was the mainstay of Howard's career, a place where he could experiment with new story forms and ideas. Howard frequently crossed genres, and because of the magazine's loosely defined theme and generous reader comments in every issue, he was able to get a sense of what worked and what didn't. Many of those readers who commented about Howard's work were fellow authors, and the ringleader of these *Weird Tales* writers was H. P. Lovecraft. A recluse living in Providence, Rhode Island, he kept a voluminous correspondence with authors, poets, and fans, and through this correspondence was a tremendous influence on a generation of writers, including Robert E. Howard.

Their correspondence and friendship is legendary. Through the initial fan letter that Lovecraft sent Howard, Howard was able to meet and correspond with Clark Ashton Smith, August Derleth, and other members of what would eventually be known as "The Lovecraft Circle." They traded poetry and drawings, shared stories with one another, and talked about the craft of writing, when they weren't arguing politics or recommending books. These isolated authors in other states became Howard's peers and friends, praising his work and encouraging him to do more of it. They were as influential on Howard as Howard was on them.

The book in your hands is the first of a ten-volume set that collects the fantasy, horror, weird and sword-and-sorcery stories that Howard published in *Weird Tales* and elsewhere, in the order that they appeared. While not strictly in the order that Howard wrote them, they are valuable in that it gives us a picture of how quickly he improved. Each story builds on the last one, bringing with it whatever worked from the previous endeavor. "Spear and Fang," for example, is a straightforward action piece. Howard kept the fast action in "In the Forest of Villfere," changed the historical setting and turned it into a traditional supernatural story. This worked so well that one of the characters in "Villefere" makes a return appearance in "Wolfshead," a tightly plotted period piece with action aplenty and the first story to net Howard the coveted cover art for that issue. The historical setting would soon reappear in the afore-mentioned "Red Shadows," along with a sword-wielding hero, supernatural happenings, and a spectacular fight at the end. With "Red Shadows," Howard had all of the makings of his signature style in place; a driving plot, memorable characters, brisk action, and poetically rendered prose that leapt off of the page.

Many readers overlook Howard's poetry and they do so at their own peril. Howard was an excellent poet; he wrote poetry throughout his career, in a variety of styles. Supernatural, macabre, and otherworldly, Howard's poems all tell fascinating stories. They are especially effective if read aloud. One of the keys to Howard's effectiveness as a writer was his use of poetical structures in his prose fiction. Repetitive sounds, cadenced rhythms, and succinct word choices are all a part of Howard's easy-to-recognize, impossible-to-duplicate style.

Even a casual reader will be amazed at how quickly Howard developed as a writer of fiction. You will witness a miraculous transformation as you read these stories, just as the first ever Robert E. Howard fans got to read them. I can just imagine someone reading King Kull for the first time and thinking, "Boy, this is as good as it gets!" and then reading the first Conan story, "The Phoenix on the Sword" three years later. And Howard got better after that. Incredible.

Weird Tales was Howard's literary home. He felt comfortable enough within its hallowed pages to break new ground and try new things. Howard found colleagues and friends in the other *Weird Tales* writers who shared his interests and stimulated his creativity. He received encouragement and feedback from Farnsworth Wright, the fans, and his fellow authors. *Weird Tales* was the anvil on which Howard forged the sword of his literary legacy. These stories are that legacy. Enjoy!

— Mark Finn
July, 2004
Austin, Texas

SPEAR AND FANG

Weird Tales, July 1925

A-aea crouched close to the cave mouth, watching Ga-nor with wondering eyes. Ga-nor's occupation interested her, as well as Ga-nor himself. As for Ga-nor, he was too occupied with his work to notice her. A torch stuck in a niche in the cave wall dimly illuminated the roomy cavern, and by its light Ga-nor was laboriously tracing figures on the wall. With a piece of flint he scratched the outline and then with a twig dipped in ocher paint completed the figure. The result was crude, but grave evidence of real artistic genius, struggling for expression.

It was a mammoth that he sought to depict, and little A-aea's eyes widened with wonder and admiration. Wonderful! What though the beast lacked a leg and had no tail? It was tribesmen, just struggling out of utter barbarism, who were the critics, and to them Ga-nor was a past master.

However, it was not to watch the reproduction of a mammoth that A-aea hid among the scanty bushes by Ga-nor's cave. The admiration for the painting paled beside the look of positive adoration with which she favored the artist. Indeed, Ga-nor was not unpleasing to the eye. Tall he was, towering well over six feet, leanly built, with mighty shoulders and narrow hips, the build of a fighting man. Both his hands and his feet were long and slim; and his features, thrown into bold profile by the flickering torch-light, were intelligent, with a high, broad forehead, topped by a mane of sandy hair.

A-aea herself was very easy to look upon. Her hair, as well as her eyes, was black and fell about her slim shoulders in a rippling wave. No ocher tattooing tinted her cheek, for she was still unmated.

Both the girl and the youth were perfect specimens of the great Cro-Magnon race which came from no man knows where and announced and enforced their supremacy over beast and beast-man.

A-aea glanced about nervously. All ideas to the contrary, customs and taboos are much more narrow and vigorously enforced among savage peoples.

The more primitive a race, the more intolerant their customs. Vice and licentiousness may be the rule, but the appearance of vice is shunned and condemned. So if A-aea had been discovered, hiding near the cave of an unattached young man, denunciation as a shameless woman would have been her lot, and doubtless a public whipping.

To be proper, A-aea should have played the modest, demure maiden, perhaps skillfully arousing the young artist's interest without seeming to do so. Then, if the youth was pleased, would have followed public wooing by means of crude love-songs and music from reed pipes. Then barter with her parents and then — marriage. Or no wooing at all, if the lover was wealthy.

But little A-aea was herself a mark of progress. Covert glances had failed to attract the attention of the young man who seemed engrossed with his artistry, so she had taken to the unconventional way of spying upon him, in hopes of finding some way to win him.

Ga-nor turned from his completed work, stretched and glanced toward the cave mouth. Like a frightened rabbit, little A-aea ducked and darted away.

When Ga-nor emerged from the cave, he was puzzled by the sight of a small, slender footprint in the soft loam outside the cave.

A-aea walked primly toward her own cave, which was, with most of the others, at some distance from Ga-nor's cave. As she did so, she noticed a group of warriors talking excitedly in front of the chief's cave.

A mere girl might not intrude upon the councils of men, but such was A-aea's curiosity, that she dared a scolding by slipping nearer. She heard the words "footprint" and "gur-na" (man-ape).

The footprints of a gur-na had been found in the forest, not far from the caves.

"Gur-na" was a word of hatred and horror to the people of the caves, for creatures whom the tribesmen called "gur-na", or man-apes, were the hairy monsters of another age, the brutish men of the Neandertal. More feared than mammoth or tiger, they had ruled the forests until the Cro-Magnon men had come and waged savage warfare against them. Of mighty power and little mind, savage, bestial and cannibalistic, they inspired the tribesmen with loathing and horror — a horror transmitted through the ages in tales of ogres and goblins, of werewolves and beast-men.

They were fewer and more cunning, now. No longer they rushed roaring to battle, but cunning and frightful, they slunk about the forests, the terror of all beasts, brooding in their brutish minds with hatred for the men who had driven them from the best hunting grounds.

And ever the Cro-Magnon men trailed them down and slaughtered them, until sullenly they had withdrawn far into the deep forests. But the fear of them remained with the tribesmen, and no woman went into the jungle alone.

Sometimes children went, and sometimes they returned not; and searchers found but signs of a ghastly feast, with tracks that were not the tracks of beasts, nor yet the tracks of men.

And so a hunting party would go forth and hunt the monster down. Sometimes it gave battle and was slain, and sometimes it fled before them and escaped into the depths of the forest, where they dared not follow. Once a hunting party, reckless with the chase, had pursued a fleeing gur-na into the deep forest and there, in a deep ravine, where overhanging limbs shut out the sunlight, numbers of the Neandertalers had come upon them.

So no more entered the forests.

A-aea turned away, with a glance at the forest. Somewhere in its depths lurked the beast-man, piggish eyes glinting crafty hate, malevolent, frightful.

Someone stepped across her path. It was Ka-nanu, the son of a councilor of the chief.

She drew away with a shrug of her shoulders. She did not like Ka-nanu and she was afraid of him. He wooed her with a mocking air, as if he did it merely for amusement and would take her whenever he wished, anyway. He seized her by the wrist.

"Turn not away, fair maiden," said he. "It is your slave, Ka-nanu."

"Let me go," she answered. "I must go to the spring for water."

"Then I will go with you, moon of delight, so that no beast may harm you."

And accompany her he did, in spite of her protests.

"There is a gur-na abroad," he told her sternly. "It is lawful for a man to accompany even an unmated maiden, for protection. And I am Ka-nanu," he added, in a different tone; "do not resist me too far, or I will teach you obedience."

A-aea knew somewhat of the man's ruthless nature. Many of the tribal girls looked with favor on Ka-nanu, for he was bigger and taller even than Ga-nor, and more handsome in a reckless, cruel way. But A-aea loved Ga-nor and she was afraid of Ka-nanu. Her very fear of him kept her from resisting his approaches too much. Ga-nor was known to be gentle with women, if careless of them, while Ka-nanu, thereby showing himself to be another mark of progress, was proud or his success with women and used his power over them in no gentle fashion.

A-aea found Ka-nanu was to be feared more than a beast, for at the spring just out of sight of the caves, he seized her in his arms.

"A-aea," he whispered, "my little antelope, I have you at last. You shall not escape me."

In vain she struggled and pleaded with him. Lifting her in his mighty arms he strode away into the forest.

Frantically she strove to escape, to dissuade him.

"I am not powerful enough to resist you," she said, "but I will accuse you before the tribe."

"You will never accuse me, little antelope," he said, and she read another, even more sinister intention in his cruel countenance.

On and on into the forest he carried her, and in the midst of a glade he paused, his hunter's instinct alert.

From the trees in front of them dropped a hideous monster, a hairy, misshapen, frightful thing.

A-aea's scream re-echoed through the forest, as the thing approached. Ka-nanu, white-lipped and horrified, dropped A-aea to the ground and told her to run. Then, drawing knife and ax, he advanced.

The Neandertal man plunged forward on short, gnarled legs. He was covered with hair and his features were more hideous than an ape's because of the grotesque quality of the man in them. Flat, flaring nostrils, retreating chin, fangs, no forehead whatever, great, immensely long arms dangling from sloping, incredible shoulders, the monster seemed like the devil himself to the terrified girl. His apelike head came scarcely to Ka-nanu's shoulders, yet he must have outweighed the warrior by nearly a hundred pounds.

On he came like a charging buffalo, and Ka-nanu met him squarely and boldly. With flint ax and obsidian dagger he thrust and smote, but the ax was brushed aside like a toy and the arm that held the knife snapped like a stick in the misshapen hand of the Neandertaler. The girl saw the councilor's son wrenched from the ground and swung into the air, saw him hurled clear across the glade, saw the monster leap after him and rend him limb from limb.

Then the Neandertaler turned his attention to her. A new expression came into his hideous eyes as he lumbered toward her, his great hairy hands horridly smeared with blood, reaching toward her.

Unable to flee, she lay dizzy with horror and fear. And the monster dragged her to him, leering into her eyes. He swung her over his shoulder and waddled away through the trees; and the girl, half-fainting, knew that he was taking her to his lair, where no man would dare come to rescue her.

Ga-nor came down to the spring to drink. Idly he noticed the faint footprints of a couple who had come before him. Idly he noticed that they had not returned.

Each footprint had its individual characteristic. That of the man he knew to be Ka-nanu. The other track was the same as that in front of his cave. He wondered, idly as Ga-nor was wont to do all things except the painting of pictures.

Then, at the spring, he noticed that the footprints of the girl ceased, but that the man's turned toward the jungle and were more deeply imprinted than before. Therefore Ka-nanu was carrying the girl.

Ga-nor was no fool. He knew that a man carries a girl into the forest for no good purpose. If she had been willing to go, she would not have been carried.

Now Ga-nor (another mark of progress) was inclined to meddle in things not pertaining to him. Perhaps another man would have shrugged his shoulders and gone his way, reflecting that it would not be well to interfere with a son of a councilor. But Ga-nor had few interests, and once his interest was roused he was inclined to see a thing through. Moreover, though not renowned as a fighter, he feared no man.

Therefore, he loosened ax and dagger in his belt, shifted his grip on his spear, and took up the trail.

On and on, deeper and deeper into the forest, the Neandertaler carried little A-aea.

The forest was silent and evil, no birds, no insects broke the stillness. Through the overhanging trees no sunlight filtered. On padded feet that made no noise the Neandertaler hurried on.

Beasts slunk out of his path. Once a great python came slithering through the jungle and the Neandertaler took to the trees with surprising speed for one of his gigantic bulk. He was not at home in the trees, however, not even as much as A-aea would have been.

Once or twice the girl glimpsed another such monster as her captor. Evidently they had gone far beyond the vaguely defined boundaries of her race. The other Neandertal men avoided them. It was evident that they lived as do beasts, uniting only against some common enemy and not often then. Therein had lain the reason for the success of the Cro-Magnons' warfare against them.

Into a ravine he carried the girl, and into a cave, small and vaguely illumined by the light from without. He threw her roughly to the floor of the cave, where she lay, too terrified to rise.

The monster watched her, like some demon of the forest. He did not even jabber at her, as an ape would have done. The Neandertalers had no form of speech whatever.

He offered her meat of some kind — uncooked, of course. Her mind reeling with horror, she saw that it was the arm of a Cro-Magnon child. When he saw she would not eat, he devoured it himself, tearing the flesh with great fangs.

He took her between his great hands, bruising her soft flesh. He ran rough fingers through her hair, and when he saw that he hurt her he seemed filled with a fiendish glee. He tore out handfuls of her hair, seeming to enjoy devilishly the torturing of his fair captive. A-aea set her teeth and would not scream as she had done at first, and presently he desisted.

The leopard-skin garment she wore seemed to enrage him. The leopard was his hereditary foe. He plucked it from her and tore it to pieces.

And meanwhile Ga-nor was hurrying through the forest. He was racing now, and his face was a devil's mask, for he had come upon the bloody glade and found the monster's tracks, leading away from it.

And in the cave in the ravine the Neandertaler reached for A-aea.

She sprang back and he plunged toward her. He had her in a corner but she slipped under his arm and sprang away. He was still between her and the outside of the cave.

Unless she could get past him, he would corner her and seize her. So she pretended to spring to one side. The Neandertaler lumbered in that direction, and quick as a cat she sprang the other way and darted past him, out into the ravine.

With a bellow he charged after her. A stone rolled beneath her foot, flinging her headlong; before she could rise his hand seized her shoulder. As he dragged her into the cave, she screamed, wildly, frenziedly, with no hope of rescue, just the scream of a woman in the grasp of a beast.

Ga-nor heard that scream as he bounded down into the ravine. He approached the cave swiftly but cautiously. As he looked in, he saw red rage. In the vague light of the cave, the great Neandertaler stood, his piggish eyes on his foe, hideous, hairy, blood-smeared, while at his feet, her soft white body contrasting with the shaggy monster, her long hair gripped in his blood-stained hand, lay A-aea.

The Neandertaler bellowed, dropped his captive and charged. And Ga-nor met him, not matching brute strength with his lesser might, but leaping back and out of the cave. His spear leaped and the monster bellowed as it tore through his arm. Leaping back again, the warrior jerked his spear and crouched. Again the Neandertaler rushed, and again the warrior leaped away and thrust, this time for the great hairy chest. And so they battled, speed and intelligence against brute strength and savagery.

Once the great, lashing arm of the monster caught Ga-nor upon the shoulder and hurled him a dozen feet away, rendering that arm nearly useless for a time. The Neandertaler bounded after him, but Ga-nor flung himself to one side and leaped to his feet. Again and again his spear drew blood, but apparently it seemed only to enrage the monster.

Then before the warrior knew it, the wall of the ravine was at his back and he heard A-aea shriek as the monster rushed in. The spear was torn from his hand and he was in the grasp of his foe. The great arms encircled his neck and shoulders, the great fangs sought his throat. He thrust his elbow under the retreating chin of his antagonist, and with his free hand struck the hideous face again and again; blows that would have felled an ordinary man but which the Neandertal beast did not even notice.

Ga-nor felt consciousness going from him. The terrific arms were crushing him, threatening to break his neck. Over the shoulder of his foe he saw the girl approaching with a great stone, and he tried to motion her back.

With a great effort he reached down over the monster's arm and found his ax. But so close were they clinched together that he could not draw it. The Neandertal man set himself to break his foe to pieces as one breaks a stick. But Ga-nor's elbow was thrust under his chin, and the more the Neandertal man tugged, the deeper drove the elbow into this hairy throat. Presently he realized that fact and flung Ga-nor away from him. As he did so, the warrior drew his ax, and striking with the fury of desperation, clove the monster's head.

For a minute Ga-nor stood reeling above his foe, then he felt a soft form within his arms and saw a pretty face, close to his.

"Ga-nor!" A-aea whispered, and Ga-nor gathered the girl in his arms.

"What I have fought for I will keep," said he.

And so it was that the girl who went forth into the forest in the arms of an abductor came back in the arms of a lover and a mate.

IN THE FOREST OF VILLEFORE

Weird Tales, August 1925

The sun had set. The great shadows came striding over the forest. In the weird twilight of a late summer day, I saw the path ahead glide on among the mighty trees and disappear. And I shuddered and glanced fearfully over my shoulder. Miles behind lay the nearest village — miles ahead the next.

I looked to left and to right as I strode on, and anon I looked behind me. And anon I stopped short, grasping my rapier, as a breaking twig betokened the going of some small beast. Or was it a beast?

But the path led on and I followed, because, forsooth, I had naught else to do.

As I went I bethought me, "My own thoughts will route me, if I be not aware. What is there in this forest, except perhaps the creatures that roam it, deer and the like? Tush, the foolish legends of those villagers!"

And so I went and the twilight faded into dusk. Stars began to blink and the leaves of the trees murmured in the faint breeze. And then I stopped short, my sword leaping to my hand, for just ahead, around a curve of the path, someone was singing. The words I could not distinguish, but the accent was strange, almost barbaric.

I stepped behind a great tree, and the cold sweat beaded my forehead. Then the singer came in sight, a tall, thin man, vague in the twilight. I shrugged my shoulders. A *man* I did not fear. I sprang out, my point raised.

"Stand!"

He showed no surprise. "I prithee, handle thy blade with care, friend," he said.

Somewhat ashamed, I lowered my sword.

"I am new to this forest," I quoth, apologetically. "I heard talk of bandits. I crave pardon. Where lies the road to VillefPre?"

"*Corbleu*, you've missed it," he answered. "You should have branched off to the right some distance back. I am going there myself. If you may abide my company, I will direct you."

I hesitated. Yet why should I hesitate?

"Why, certainly. My name is de Montour, of Normandy."

"And I am Carolus le Loup."

"No!" I started back.

He looked at me in astonishment.

"Pardon," said I; "the name is strange. Does not *loup* mean wolf?"

"My family were always great hunters," he answered. He did not offer his hand.

"You will pardon my staring," said I as we walked down the path, "but I can hardly see your face in the dusk."

I sensed that he was laughing, though he made no sound.

"It is little to look upon," he answered.

I stepped closer and then leaped away, my hair bristling.

"A mask!" I exclaimed. "Why do you wear a mask, *m'sieu?*"

"It is a vow," he exclaimed. "In fleeing a pack of hounds I vowed that if I escaped I would wear a mask for a certain time."

"Hounds, *m'sieu?*"

"Wolves," he answered quickly; "I said wolves."

We walked in silence for awhile and then my companion said, "I am surprised that you walk these woods by night. Few people come these ways even in the day."

"I am in haste to reach the border," I answered. "A treaty has been signed with the English, and the Duke of Burgundy should know of it. The people at the village sought to dissuade me. They spoke of — a wolf that was purported to roam these woods."

"Here the path branches to VillefPre," said he, and I saw a narrow, crooked path that I had not seen when I passed it before. It led in amid the darkness of the trees. I shuddered.

"You wish to return to the village?"

"No!" I exclaimed. "No, no! Lead on."

So narrow was the path that we walked single file, he leading. I looked well at him. He was taller, much taller than I, and thin, wiry. He was dressed in a costume that smacked of Spain. A long rapier swung at his hip. He walked with long easy strides, noiselessly.

Then he began to talk of travel and adventure. He spoke of many lands and seas he had seen and many strange things. So we talked and went farther and farther into the forest.

I presumed that he was French, and yet he had a very strange accent, that was neither French nor Spanish nor English, not like any language I had ever heard. Some words he slurred strangely and some he could not pronounce at all.

"This path is often used, is it?" I asked.

"Not by many," he answered and laughed silently. I shuddered. It was very dark and the leaves whispered together among the branches.

"A fiend haunts this forest," I said.

"So the peasants say," he answered, "but I have roamed it oft and have never seen his face."

Then he began to speak of strange creatures of darkness, and the moon rose and shadows glided among the trees. He looked up at the moon.

"Haste!" said he. "We must reach our destination before the moon reaches her zenith."

We hurried along the trail.

"They say," said I, "that a werewolf haunts these woodlands."

"It might be," said he, and we argued much upon the subject.

"The old women say," said he, "that if a werewolf is slain while a wolf, then he is slain, but if he is slain as a man, then his half-soul will haunt his slayer forever. But haste thee, the moon nears her zenith."

We came into a small moonlit glade and the stranger stopped.

"Let us pause a while," said he.

"Nay, let us be gone," I urged; "I like not this place."

He laughed without sound. "Why," said he, "This is a fair glade. As good as a banquet hall it is, and many times have I feasted here. Ha, ha, ha! Look ye, I will show you a dance." And he began bounding here and there, anon flinging back his head and laughing silently. Thought I, the man is mad.

As he danced his weird dance I looked about me. *The trail went not on but stopped in the glade.*

"Come," said I "we must on. Do you not smell the rank, hairy scent that hovers about the glade? Wolves den here. Perhaps they are about us and are gliding upon us even now."

He dropped upon all fours, bounded higher than my head, and came toward me with a strange slinking motion.

"That dance is called the Dance of the Wolf," said he, and my hair bristled.

"Keep off!" I stepped back, and with a screech that set the echoes shuddering he leaped for me, and though a sword hung at his belt he did not draw it. My rapier was half out when he grasped my arm and flung me headlong. I dragged him with me and we struck the ground together. Wrenching a hand free I jerked off the mask. A shriek of horror broke from my lips. Beast eyes glittered beneath that mask, white fangs flashed in the moonlight. *The face was that of a wolf.*

In an instant those fangs were at my throat. Taloned hands tore the sword from my grasp. I beat at that horrible face with my clenched fists, but his jaws were fastened on my shoulders, his talons tore at my throat. Then I was on my back. The world was fading. Blindly I struck out. My hand dropped, then closed automatically about the hilt of my dagger, which I had been unable to get at. I drew and stabbed. A terrible, half-bestial bellowing screech. Then I reeled to my feet, free. At my feet lay the werewolf.

I stooped, raised the dagger, then paused, looked up. The moon hovered close to her zenith. *If I slew the thing as a man its frightful spirit would haunt me forever.* I sat down waiting. The *thing* watched me with flaming wolf eyes. The long wiry limbs seemed to shrink, to crook; hair seemed to grow upon them. Fearing madness, I snatched up the *thing's* own sword and hacked it to pieces. Then I flung the sword away and fled.

WOLFSHEAD

Weird Tales, April 1926

Fear? Your pardon, *Messieurs*, but the meaning of fear you do not know. No, I hold to my statement. You are soldiers, adventurers. You have known the charges of regiments of dragoons, the frenzy of wind-lashed seas. But fear, real hair-raising, horror-crawling fear, you have not known. I myself have known such fear; but until the legions of darkness swirl from Hell's gate and the world flames to ruin, will never such fear again be known to men.

Hark, I will tell you the tale; for it was many years ago and half-across the world, and none of you will ever see the man of whom I tell you, or seeing, know.

Return, then, with me across the years to a day when I, a reckless young cavalier, stepped from the small boat that had landed me from the ship floating in the harbor, cursed the mud that littered the crude wharf, and strode up the landing toward the castle, in answer to the invitation of an old friend, Dom Vincente da Lusto.

Dom Vincente was a strange, far-sighted man — a strong man, one who saw visions beyond the ken of his time. In his veins, perhaps, ran the blood of those old Phoenicians who, the priests tell us, ruled the seas and built cities in far lands, in the dim ages. His plan of fortune was strange and yet successful; few men would have thought of it; fewer could have succeeded. For his estate was upon the western coast of that dark, mystic continent, that baffler of explorers — Africa.

There by a small bay had he cleared away the sullen jungle, built his castle and his storehouses, and with ruthless hand had he wrested the riches of the land. Four ships he had: three smaller craft and one great galleon. These plied between his domains and the cities of Spain, Portugal, France, and even England, laden with rare woods, ivory, slaves; the thousand strange riches that Dom Vincente had gained by trade and by conquest.

Aye, a wild venture, a wilder commerce. And yet might he have shaped an empire from the dark land, had it not been for the rat-faced Carlos, his nephew — but I run ahead of my tale.

Look, *Messieurs*, I draw a map on the table, thus, with finger dipped in wine. Here lay the small, shallow harbor, and here the wide wharves. A landing ran thus, up the slight slope with hut-like warehouses on each side, and here it stopped at a wide, shallow moat. Over it went a narrow drawbridge and then one was confronted with a high palisade of logs set in the ground. This extended entirely around the castle. The castle itself was built on the model of another, earlier age; being more for strength then beauty. Built of stone brought from a great distance; years of labor and a thousand Negroes toiling beneath the lash had reared its walls, and now, completed, it offered an almost impregnable appearance. Such was the intention of its builders, for Barbary pirates ranged the coasts, and the horror of a native uprising lurked ever near.

A space of about a half-mile on every side of the castle was kept cleared away and roads had been built through the marshy land. All this had required an immense amount of labor, but manpower was plentiful. A present to a chief, and he furnished all that was needed. And Portuguese know how to make men work!

Less than three hundred yards to the east of the castle ran a wide, shallow river, which emptied into the harbor. The name has entirely slipped my mind. It was a heathenish title and I could never lay my tongue to it.

I found that I was not the only friend invited to the castle. It seems that once a year or some such matter, Dom Vincente brought a host of jolly companions to his lonely estate and made merry for some weeks, to make up for the work and solitude of the rest of the year.

In fact, it was nearly night, and a great banquet was in progress when I entered. I was acclaimed with great delight, greeted boisterously by friends and introduced to such strangers as were there.

Entirely too weary to take much part in the revelry, I ate, drank quietly, listened to the toasts and songs, and studied the feasters.

Dom Vincente, of course, I knew, as I had been intimate with him for years; also his pretty niece, Ysabel, who was one reason I had accepted his invitation to come to that stinking wilderness. Her second cousin, Carlos, I knew and disliked — a sly, mincing fellow with a face like a mink's. Then there was my old friend, Luigi Verenza, an Italian; and his flirt of a sister, Marcita, making eyes at the men as usual. Then there was a short, stocky German who called himself Baron von Schiller; and Jean Desmarte, an out-at-the-elbows nobleman of Gascony; and Don Florenzo de Seville, a lean, dark, silent man, who called himself a Spaniard and wore a rapier nearly as long as himself.

There were others, men and women, but it was long ago and all their names and faces I do not remember.

But there was one man whose face somehow drew my gaze as an alchemist's magnet draws steel. He was a leanly built man of slightly more than medium height, dressed plainly, almost austerely, and he wore a sword almost as long as the Spaniard's.

But it was neither his clothes nor his sword which attracted my attention. It was his face. A refined, high-bred face, it was furrowed deep with lines that gave it a weary, haggard expression. Tiny scars flecked jaw and forehead as if torn by savage claws; I could have sworn the narrow gray eyes had a fleeting, haunted look in their expression at times.

I leaned over to that flirt, Marcita, and asked the name of the man, as it had slipped my mind that we had been introduced.

"De Montour, from Normandy," she answered. "A strange man. I don't think I like him."

"Then he resists your snares, my little enchantress?" I murmured, long friendship making me as immune from her anger as from her wiles. But she chose not to be angry and answered coyly, glancing from under demurely lowered lashes.

I watched de Montour much, feeling somehow a strange fascination. He ate lightly, drank much, seldom spoke, and then only to answer questions.

Presently, toasts making the rounds, I noticed his companions urging him to rise and give a health. At first he refused, then rose, upon their repeated urgings, and stood silent for a moment, goblet raised. He seemed to dominate, to overawe the group of revelers. Then with a mocking, savage laugh, he lifted the goblet above his head.

"To Solomon," he exclaimed, "who bound all devils! And thrice cursed be he for that some escaped!"

A toast and a curse in one! It was drunk silently, and with many sidelong, doubting glances.

That night I retired early, weary of the long sea voyage and my head spinning from the strength of the wine, of which Dom Vincente kept such great stores.

My room was near the top of the castle and looked out toward the forests of the south and the river. The room was furnished in crude, barbaric splendor, as was all the rest of the castle.

Going to the window, I gazed out at the arquebusier pacing the castle grounds just inside the palisade; at the cleared space lying unsightly and barren in the moonlight; at the forest beyond; at the silent river.

From the native quarter close to the river bank came the weird twanging of some rude lute, sounding a barbaric melody.

In the dark shadows of the forest some uncanny night-bird lifted a mocking voice. A thousand minor notes sounded – birds, and beasts, and the devil knows what else! Some great jungle cat began a hair-lifting yowling. I shrugged my shoulders and turned from the windows. Surely devils lurked in those somber depths.

There came a knock at my door and I opened it, to admit de Montour.

He strode to the window and gazed at the moon, which rode resplendent and glorious.

"The moon is almost full, is it not, *Monsieur*?" he remarked, turning to me. I nodded, and I could have sworn that he shuddered.

"Your pardon, *Monsieur*. I will not annoy you further." He turned to go, but at the door turned and retraced his steps.

"*Monsieur*," he almost whispered, with a fierce intensity, "whatever you do, be sure you bar and bolt your door tonight!"

Then he was gone, leaving me to stare after him bewilderedly.

I dozed off to sleep, the distant shouts of the revelers in my ears, and though I was weary, or perhaps because of it, I slept lightly. While I never really awoke until morning, sounds and noises seemed to drift to me through my veil of slumber, and once it seemed that something was prying and shoving against the bolted door.

As is to be supposed, most of the guests were in a beastly humor the following day and remained in their rooms most of the morning or else straggled down late. Besides Dom Vincente there were really only three of the masculine members sober: de Montour; the Spaniard, de Seville (as he called himself); and myself. The Spaniard never touched wine, and though de Montour consumed incredible quantities of it, it never affected him in any way.

The ladies greeted us most graciously.

"S'truth, *Signor*," remarked that minx Marcita, giving me her hand with a gracious air that was like to make me snicker, "I am glad to see there are gentlemen among us who care more for our company than for the wine cup; for most of them are most surprizingly befuddled this morning."

Then with a most outrageous turning of her wondrous eyes, "Methinks someone was too drunk to be discreet last night — or not drunk enough. For unless my poor senses deceive me much, someone came fumbling at my door late in the night."

"Ha!" I exclaimed in quick anger, "some —!"

"No. Hush." She glanced about as if to see that we were alone, then: "Is it not strange that Signor de Montour, before he retired last night, instructed me to fasten my door firmly?"

"Strange," I murmured, but did not tell her that he had told me the same thing.

"And is it not strange, Pierre, that though Signor de Montour left the banquet hall even before you did, yet he has the appearance of one who has been up all night?"

I shrugged. A woman's fancies are often strange.

"Tonight," she said roguishly, "I will leave my door unbolted and see whom I catch."

"You will do no such thing."

She showed her little teeth in a contemptuous smile and displayed a small, wicked dagger.

"Listen, imp. De Montour gave me the same warning he did you. Whatever he knew, whoever prowled the halls last night, the object was more apt murder than amorous adventure. Keep you your doors bolted. The lady Ysabel shares your room, does she not?"

"Not she. And I send my woman to the slave quarters at night," she murmured, gazing mischievously at me from beneath drooping eyelids.

"One would think you a girl of no character from your talk," I told her, with the frankness of youth and of long friendship. "Walk with care, young lady, else I tell your brother to spank you."

And I walked away to pay my respects to Ysabel. The Portuguese girl was the very opposite of Marcita, being a shy, modest young thing, not so beautiful as the Italian, but exquisitely pretty in an appealing, almost childish air. I once had thoughts — Hi ho! To be young and foolish!

Your pardon, *Messieurs*. An old man's mind wanders. It was of de Montour that I meant to tell you — de Montour and Dom Vincente's mink-faced cousin.

A band of armed natives were thronged about the gates, kept at a distance by the Portuguese soldiers. Among them were some score of young men and women all naked, chained neck to neck. Slaves they were, captured by some warlike tribe and brought for sale. Dom Vincente looked them over personally.

Followed a long haggling and bartering, of which I quickly wearied and turned away, wondering that a man of Dom Vincente's rank could so demean himself as to stoop to trade.

But I strolled back when one of the natives of the village nearby came up and interrupted the sale with a long harangue to Dom Vincente.

While they talked de Montour came up, and presently Dom Vincente turned to us and said, "One of the woodcutters of the village was torn to pieces by a leopard or some such beast last night. A strong young man and unmarried."

"A leopard? Did they see it?" suddenly asked de Montour, and when Dom Vincente said no, that it came and went in the night, de Montour lifted a trembling hand and drew it across his forehead, as if to brush away cold sweat.

"Look you, Pierre," quoth Dom Vincente, "I have here a slave who, wonder of wonders, desires to be your man. Though the devil only knows why."

He led up a slim young Jakri, a mere youth, whose main asset seemed a merry grin.

"He is yours," said Dom Vincente. "He is goodly trained and will make a fine servant. And look ye, a slave is of an advantage over a servant, for all he requires is food and a loincloth or so with a touch of the whip to keep him in his place."

It was not long before I learned why Gola wished to be "my man," choosing me among all the rest. It was because of my hair. Like many dandies of that day, I wore it long and curled, the strands falling to my shoulders. As it happened, I was the only man of the party who so wore my hair, and Gola would sit and gaze at it in silent admiration for hours at a time, or until, growing nervous under his unblinking scrutiny, I would boot him forth.

It was that night that a brooding animosity, hardly apparent, between Baron von Schiller and Jean Desmarte broke out into a flame.

As usual, a woman was the cause. Marcita carried on a most outrageous flirtation with both of them.

That was not wise. Desmarte was a wild young fool. Von

Schiller was a lustful beast. But when, *Messieurs*, did woman ever use wisdom?

Their hate flamed to a murderous fury when the German sought to kiss Marcita.

Swords were clashing in an instant. But before Dom Vincente could thunder a command to halt, Luigi was between the combatants, and had beaten their swords down, hurling them back viciously.

"Signori," said he softly, but with a fierce intensity, "is it the part of high-bred *signori* to fight over my sister? Ha, by the toenails of Satan, for the toss of a coin I would call you both out! You, Marcita, go to your chamber, instantly, nor leave until I give you permission."

And she went, for, independent though she was, none cared to face the slim, effeminate-appearing youth when a tigerish snarl curled his lips, a murderous gleam lightened his dark eyes.

Apologies were made, but from the glances the two rivals threw at each other, we knew that the quarrel was not forgotten and would blaze forth again at the slightest pretext.

Late that night I woke suddenly with a strange, eerie feeling of horror. Why, I could not say. I rose, saw that the door was firmly bolted, and seeing Gola asleep on the floor, kicked him awake irritably.

And just as he got up, hastily, rubbing himself, the silence was broken by a wild scream, a scream that rang through the castle and brought a startled shout from the arquebusier pacing the palisade; a scream from the mouth of a girl, frenzied with terror.

Gola squawked and dived behind the divan. I jerked the door open and raced down the dark corridor. Dashing down a winding stair, I caromed into someone at the bottom and we tumbled headlong.

He gasped something and I recognized the voice of Jean Desmarte. I hauled him to his feet, and raced along, he following; the screams had ceased, but the whole castle was in an uproar, voices shouting, the clank of weapons, lights flashing up, Dom Vincente's voice shouting for the soldiers, the noise of armed men rushing through the rooms and falling over each other. With all the confusion, Desmarte, the Spaniard, and I reached Marcita's room just as Luigi darted inside and snatched his sister into his arms.

Others rushed in, carrying lights and weapons, shouting, demanding to know what was occurring.

The girl lay quietly in her brother's arms, her dark hair loose and rippling over her shoulders, her dainty night-garments torn to shreds and exposing her lovely body. Long scratches showed upon her arms, breasts and shoulders.

Presently, she opened her eyes, shuddered, then shrieked wildly and clung frantically to Luigi, begging him not to let something take her.

"The door!" she whimpered. "I left it unbarred. And *something* crept into my room through the darkness. I struck at it with my dagger and it hurled me to the floor, tearing, tearing at me. Then I fainted."

"Where is von Schiller?" asked the Spaniard, a fierce glint in his dark eyes. Every man glanced at his neighbor. All the guests were there except the German. I noted de Montour gazing at the terrified girl, his face more haggard than usual. And I thought it strange that he wore no weapon.

"Aye, von Schiller!" exclaimed Desmarte fiercely. And half of us followed Dom Vincente out into the corridor. We began a vengeful search through the castle, and in a small, dark hallway we found von Schiller. On his face he lay, in a crimson, ever-widening stain.

"This is the work of some native!" exclaimed Desmarte, face aghast.

"Nonsense," bellowed Dom Vincente. "No native from the outside could pass the soldiers. All slaves, von Schiller's among them, were barred and bolted in the slave quarters, except Gola, who sleeps in Pierre's room, and Ysabel's woman."

"But who else could have done this deed?" exclaimed Desmarte in a fury.

"You!" I said abruptly; "else why ran you so swiftly away from the room of Marcita?"

"Curse you, you lie!" he shouted, and his swift-drawn sword leaped for my breast; but quick as he was, the Spaniard was quicker. Desmarte's rapier clattered against the wall and Desmarte stood like a statue, the Spaniard's motionless point just touching his throat.

"Bind him," said the Spaniard without passion.

"Put down your blade, Don Florenzo," commanded Dom Vincente, striding forward and dominating the scene. "Signor Desmarte, you are one of my best friends, but I am the only law here and duty must be done. Give your word that you will not seek to escape."

"I give it," replied the Gascon calmly. "I acted hastily. I apologize. I was not intentionally running away, but the halls and corridors of this cursed castle confuse me."

Of us all, probably but one man believed him.

"Messieurs!" De Montour stepped forward. "This youth is not guilty. Turn the German over."

Two soldiers did as he asked. De Montour shuddered, pointing. The rest of us glanced once, then recoiled in horror.

"Could man have done that thing?"

"With a dagger —" began someone.

"No dagger makes wounds like that," said the Spaniard. "The German was torn to pieces by the talons of some frightful beast."

We glanced about us, half-expecting some hideous monster to leap upon us from the shadows.

We searched that castle; every foot, every inch of it. And we found no trace of any beast.

Dawn was breaking when I returned to my room, to find that Gola had barred himself in; and it took me nearly a half-hour to convince him to let me in.

Having smacked him soundly and berated him for his cowardice, I told him what had taken place, as he could understand French and could speak a weird mixture which he proudly called French.

His mouth gaped and only the whites of his eyes showed as the tale reached its climax.

"Ju ju!" he whispered fearsomely. "Fetish man!"

Suddenly an idea came to me. I had heard vague tales, little more than hints of legends, of the devilish leopard cult that existed on the West Coast. No white man had ever seen one of its votaries, but Dom Vincente had told us tales of beast-men, disguised in skins of leopards, who stole through the midnight jungle and slew and devoured. A ghastly thrill traveled up and down my spine and in an instant I had Gola in a grasp which made him yell.

"Was that a leopard-man?" I hissed, shaking him viciously.

"Massa, massa!" he gasped. "Me good boy! Ju ju man get! More besser no tell!"

"You'll tell me!" I gritted, renewing my endeavors, until, his hands waving feeble protests, he promised to tell me what he knew.

"No leopard-man!" he whispered, and his eyes grew big with supernatural fear. "Moon, he full, woodcutter find, him heap clawed. Find 'nother woodcutter. Big Massa (Dom Vincente) say, 'leopard.' No leopard. But leopard-man, he come to kill. *Something kill leopard-man!* Heap claw! Hai, hai! Moon full again. Something come in lonely hut; claw um woman, claw um pick'nin. Man find um claw up. Big Massa say 'leopard.' Full moon again. Something come in lonely hut; claw um woman, claw um pick'nin. Man find um claw up. Big Massa say 'leopard.' Full moon again, and wood-cutter find, heap clawed. Now come in castle. No leopard. *But always footmarks of a man!*"

I gave a startled, incredulous exclamation.

It was true, Gola averred. Always the footprints of a man led away from the scene of the murder. Then why did the natives not tell the Big Massa that he might hunt down the fiend? Here Gola assumed a crafty expression and whispered in my ear, *the footprints were of a man who wore shoes!*

Even assuming that Gola was lying, I felt a thrill of unexplainable horror. Who, then, did the natives believe was doing these frightful murders?

And he answered: Dom Vincente!

By this time, *Messieurs*, my mind was in a whirl.

What was the meaning of all this? Who slew the German and sought to ravish Marcita? And as I reviewed the crime, it appeared to me that murder rather than rape was the object of the attack.

Why did de Montour warn us, and then appear to have knowledge of the crime, telling us that Desmarte was innocent and then proving it?

It was all beyond me.

The tale of the slaughter got among the natives, in spite of all we could do, and they appeared restless and nervous, and thrice that day Dom Vincente had a black lashed for insolence. A brooding atmosphere pervaded the castle.

I considered going to Dom Vincente with Gola's tale, but decided to wait awhile.

The women kept to their chambers that day, the men were restless and moody. Dom Vincente announced that the sentries would be doubled and some would patrol the corridors of the castle itself. I found myself musing cynically that if Gola's suspicions were true, sentries would be of little good.

I am not, *Messieurs*, a man to brook such a situation with patience. And I was young then. So as we drank before retiring, I flung my goblet on the table and angrily announced that in spite of man, beast or devil, I slept that night with doors flung wide. And I tramped angrily to my chamber.

Again, as on the first night, de Montour came. And his face was as a man who has looked into the gaping gates of Hell.

"I have come," he said, "to ask you — nay, *Monsieur*, to implore you — to reconsider your rash determination."

I shook my head impatiently.

"You are resolved? Yes? Then I ask you to do this for me, that after I enter my chamber, you will bolt my doors from the outside."

I did as he asked, and then made my way back to my chamber, my mind in a maze of wonderment. I had sent Gola to the slave quarters, and I laid rapier and dagger close at hand. Nor did I go to bed, but crouched in a great chair, in the darkness. Then I had much ado to keep from sleeping. To keep myself awake, I fell to musing on the strange words of de Montour. He seemed to be laboring under great excitement; his eyes hinted of ghastly mysteries known to him alone. And yet his face was not that of a wicked man.

Suddenly the notion took me to go to his chamber and talk with him.

Walking those dark passages was a shuddersome task, but eventually I stood before de Montour's door. I called softly. Silence. I reached out a hand and felt splintered fragments of wood. Hastily I struck flint and steel which I carried, and the flaming tinder showed the great oaken door sagging on its mighty hinges; showed a door smashed and splintered *from the inside*. And the chamber of de Montour was unoccupied.

Some instinct prompted me to hurry back to my room, swiftly but silently, shoeless feet treading softly. And as I neared the door, I was aware of something in the darkness before me. Something which crept in from a side corridor and glided stealthily along.

In a wild panic of fear I leaped, striking wildly and aimlessly in the darkness. My clenched fist encountered a human head, and something went down with a crash. Again I struck alight; a man lay senseless on the floor, and he was de Montour.

I thrust a candle into a niche in the wall, and just then de Montour's eyes opened and he rose uncertainly.

"You!" I exclaimed, hardly knowing what I said. "You, of all men!"

He merely nodded.

"You killed von Schiller?"

"Yes."

I recoiled with a gasp of horror.

"Listen." He raised his hand. "Take your rapier and run me through. No man will touch you."

"No," I exclaimed. "I can not."

"Then, quick," he said hurriedly, "get into your chamber and bolt the door. Haste! It will return!"

"What will return?" I asked, with a thrill of horror. "If it will harm me, it will harm you. Come into the chamber with me."

"No, no!" he fairly shrieked, springing back from my outstretched arm. "Haste, haste! It left me for an instant, but it will return." Then in a low-pitched voice of indescribable horror: "It is returning. *It is here now!*"

And I felt a *something*, a formless, shapeless presence near. A thing of frightfulness.

De Montour was standing, legs braced, arms thrown back, fists clenched. The muscles bulged beneath his skin, his eyes widened and narrowed, the veins stood out upon his forehead as if in great physical effort. As I looked, to my horror, out of nothing, a shapeless, nameless *something* took vague form! Like a shadow it moved upon de Montour.

It was hovering about him! Good God, it was merging, becoming one with the man!

De Montour swayed; a great gasp escaped him. The dim thing vanished. De Montour wavered. Then he turned toward me, and may God grant that I never look on a face like that again!

It was a hideous, a bestial face. The eyes gleamed with a frightful ferocity; the snarling lips were drawn back from gleaming teeth, which to my startled gaze appeared more like bestial fangs than human teeth.

Silently the *thing* (I can not call it a human) slunk toward me. Gasping with horror I sprang back and through the door, just as the *thing* launched itself through the air, with a sinuous motion which even then made me think of a leaping wolf. I slammed the door, holding it against the frightful *thing* which hurled itself again and again against it.

Finally it desisted and I heard it slink stealthily off down the corridor. Faint and exhausted I sat down, waiting, listening. Through the open window wafted the breeze, bearing all the scents of Africa, the spicy and the foul. From the native village came the sound of a native drum. Other drums answered farther up the river and back in the bush. Then from somewhere in the jungle, horridly incongruous, sounded the long, high-pitched call of a timber wolf. My soul revolted.

Dawn brought a tale of terrified villagers, of a Negro woman torn by some fiend of the night, barely escaping. And to de Montour I went.

On the way I met Dom Vincente. He was perplexed and angry.

"Some hellish thing is at work in this castle," he said. "Last night, though I have said naught of it to anyone, something leaped upon the back of one of the arquebusiers, tore the leather jerkin from his shoulders and pursued him to the barbican. More, someone locked de Montour into his room last night, and he was forced to smash the door to get out."

He strode on, muttering to himself, and I proceeded down the stairs, more puzzled than ever.

De Montour sat upon a stool, gazing out the window. An indescribable air of weariness was about him.

His long hair was uncombed and tousled, his garments were tattered. With a shudder I saw faint crimson stains upon his hands, and noted that the nails were torn and broken.

He looked up as I came in, and waved me to a seat. His face was worn and haggard, but was that of a man.

After a moment's silence, he spoke.

"I will tell you my strange tale. Never before has it passed my lips, and why I tell you, knowing that you will not believe me, I can not say."

And then I listened to what was surely the wildest, the most fantastic, the weirdest tale ever heard by man.

"Years ago," said de Montour, "I was upon a military mission in northern France. Alone, I was forced to pass through the fiend-haunted woodlands of VillefPre. In those frightful forests I was beset by an inhuman, a ghastly *thing* — a werewolf. Beneath a midnight moon we fought, and I slew it. Now this is the truth: that if a werewolf is slain in the half-form of a man, its ghost will haunt its slayer through eternity. But if it is slain as a wolf, Hell gapes to receive it. The true werewolf is not (as many think) a man who may take the form of a wolf, *but a wolf who takes the form of a man!*

"Now listen, my friend, and I will tell you of the wisdom, the hellish knowledge that is mine, gained through many a frightful deed, imparted to me amid the ghastly shadows of midnight forests where fiends and half-beasts roamed.

"In the beginning, the world was strange, misshapen. Grotesque beasts wandered through its jungles. Driven from another world, ancient demons and fiends came in great numbers and settled upon this newer, younger world. Long the forces of good and evil warred.

"A strange beast, known as man, wandered among the other beasts, and since good or bad must have a concrete form ere either accomplishes its desire, the spirits of good entered man. The fiends entered other beast, reptiles and birds; and long and fiercely waged the age-old battle. But man conquered. The great dragons and serpents were slain and with them the demons. Finally, Solomon, wise beyond the ken of man, made great war upon them, and by virtue of his wisdom, slew, seized and bound. But there were some which were the fiercest, the boldest, and though Solomon drove them out he could not conquer them. Those had taken the form of wolves. As the ages passed, wolf and demon became merged. No longer could the fiend leave the body of the wolf at will. In many instances, the savagery of the wolf overcame the subtlety of the demon and enslaved him, so the wolf became again only a beast, a fierce, cunning beast, but merely a beast. But of the werewolves, there are many, even yet.

"And during the time of the full moon, the wolf may take the form, or the half-form, of a man. When the moon hovers at her zenith, however, the wolf-spirit again takes ascendancy and the werewolf becomes a true wolf once more. But if it is slain in the form of a man, then the spirit is free to haunt its slayer through the ages.

"Harken now. I had thought to have slain the *thing* after it had changed to its true shape. But I slew it an instant too soon. The moon, though it approached the zenith, had not yet reached it, nor had the *thing* taken on fully the wolf-form.

"Of this I knew nothing and went my way. But when the next

time approached for the full moon, I began to be aware of a strange, malicious influence. An atmosphere of horror hovered in the air and I was aware of inexplicable, uncanny impulses.

"One night in a small village in the center of a great forest, the influence came upon me with full power. It was night, and the moon, nearly full, was rising over the forest. And between the moon and me, I saw, floating in the upper air, ghostly and barely discernible, *the outline of a wolf's head!*

"I remember little of what happened thereafter. I remember, dimly, clambering into the silent street, remember struggling, resisting briefly, vainly, and the rest is a crimson maze, until I came to myself the next morning and found my garments and hands caked and stained crimson; and heard the horrified chattering of the villagers, telling of a pair of clandestine lovers, slaughtered in a ghastly manner, scarcely outside the village, torn to pieces as if by wild beasts, as if by wolves.

"From that village I fled aghast, but I fled not alone. In the day I could not feel the drive of my fearful captor, but when night fell and the moon rose, I ranged the silent forest, a frightful thing, a slayer of humans, a fiend in a man's body.

"God, the battles I have fought! But always it overcame me and drove me ravening after some new victim. But after the moon had passed its fullness, the *thing's* power over me ceased suddenly. Nor did it return until three nights before the moon was full again.

"Since then I have roamed the world — fleeing, fleeing, seeking to escape. Always the *thing* follows, taking possession of my body when the moon is full. Gods, the frightful deeds I have done!

"I would have slain myself long ago, but I dare not. For the soul of a suicide is accurst, and my soul would be forever hunted through the flames of Hell. And harken, most frightful of all, my slain body would forever roam the earth, moved and inhabited by the soul of the werewolf! Can any thought be more ghastly?

"And I seem immune to the weapons of man. Swords have pierced me, daggers have hacked me. I am covered with scars. Yet never have they struck me down. In Germany they bound and led me to the block. There would I have willingly placed my head, but the *thing* came upon me, and breaking my bonds, I slew and fled. Up and down the world I have wandered, leaving horror and slaughter in my trail. Chains, cells, can not hold me. The *thing* is fastened to me through all eternity.

"In desperation I accepted Dom Vincente's invitation, for look you, none knows of my frightful double life, since no one could recognize me in the clutch of the demon; and few, seeing me, live to tell of it.

"My hands are red, my soul doomed to everlasting flames, my mind is torn with remorse for my crimes. And yet I can do nothing to help myself. Surely, Pierre, no man ever knew the hell that I have known.

"Yes, I slew von Schiller, and I sought to destroy the girl Marcita. Why I did not, I can not say, for I have slain both women and men.

"Now, if you will, take your sword and slay me, and with my last breath I will give you the good God's blessing. No?

"You know now my tale and you see before you a man, fiend-haunted for all eternity."

My mind was spinning with wonderment as I left the room of de Montour. What to do, I knew not. It seemed likely that he would yet murder us all, and yet I could not bring myself to tell Dom Vincente all. From the bottom of my soul I pitied de Montour.

So I kept my peace, and in the days that followed I made occasion to seek him out and converse with him. A real friendship sprang up between us.

About this time that black devil, Gola, began to wear an air of suppressed excitement, as if he knew something he wished desperately to tell, but would not or else dared not.

So the days passed in feasting, drinking and hunting, until one night de Montour came to my chamber and pointed silently at the moon which was just rising.

"Look ye," he said, "I have a plan. I will give it out that I am going into the jungle for hunting and will go forth, apparently for several days. But at night I will return to the castle, and you must lock me into the dungeon which is used as a storeroom."

This we did, and I managed to slip down twice a day and carry food and drink to my friend. He insisted on remaining in the dungeon even in the day, for though the fiend had never exerted its influence over him in the daytime, and he believed it powerless then, yet he would take no chances.

It was during this time that I began to notice that Dom Vincente's mink-faced cousin, Carlos, was forcing his attentions upon

Ysabel, who was his second cousin, and who seemed to resent those attentions.

Myself, I would have challenged him for a duel for the toss of a coin, for I despised him, but it was really none of my affair. However, it seemed that Ysabel feared him.

My friend Luigi, by the way, had become enamored of the dainty Portuguese girl, and was making swift love to her daily.

And de Montour sat in his cell and reviewed his ghastly deeds until he battered the bars with his bare hands.

And Don Florenzo wandered about the castle grounds like a dour Mephistopheles.

And the other guests rode and quarreled and drank.

And Gola slithered about, eyeing me if always on the point of imparting momentous information. What wonder if my nerves became rasped to the shrieking point?

Each day the natives grew surlier and more and more sullen and intractable.

One night, not long before the full of the moon, I entered the dungeon where de Montour sat.

He looked up quickly.

"You dare much, coming to me in the night."

I shrugged my shoulders, seating myself.

A small barred window let in the night scents and sounds of Africa.

"Hark to the native drums," I said. "For the past week they have sounded almost incessantly."

De Montour assented.

The natives are restless. Methinks 'tis deviltry they are planning. Have you noticed that Carlos is much among them?"

"No," I answered, "but 'tis like there will be a break between him and Luigi. Luigi is paying court to Ysabel."

So we talked, when suddenly de Montour became silent and moody, answering only in monosyllables.

The moon rose and peered in at the barred windows. De Montour's face was illuminated by its beams.

And then the hand of horror grasped me. On the wall behind de Montour appeared a shadow, a shadow clearly defined of a *wolf's head!*

At the same instant de Montour felt its influence. With a shriek he bounded from his stool.

He pointed fiercely, and as with trembling hands I slammed and bolted the door behind me, I felt him hurl his weight against it. As I fled up the stairway I heard a wild raving and battering at the iron-bound door. But with all the werewolf's might the great door held.

As I entered my room, Gola dashed in and gasped out the tale he had been keeping for days.

I listened, incredulously, and then dashed forth to find Dom Vincente.

I was told that Carlos had asked him to accompany him to the village to arrange a sale of slaves.

My informer was Don Florenzo of Seville, and when I gave him a brief outline of Gola's tale, he accompanied me.

Together we dashed through the castle gate, flinging a word to the guards, and down the landing toward the village.

Dom Vincente, Dom Vincente, walk with care, keep sword loosened in its sheath! Fool, fool, to walk in the night with Carlos, the traitor!

They were nearing the village when we caught up with them. "Dom Vincente!" I exclaimed; "Return instantly to the castle. Carlos is selling you into the hands of the natives! Gola has told me that he lusts for your wealth and for Ysabel! A terrified native babbled to him of booted footprints near the places where the woodcutters were murdered, and Carlos has made the blacks believe that the slayer was you! Tonight the natives were to rise and slay every man in the castle except Carlos! Do you not believe me, Dom Vincente?"

"Is this the truth, Carlos?" asked Dom Vincente, in amaze.

Carlos laughed mockingly.

"The fool speaks truth," he said, "but it accomplishes you nothing. Ho!"

He shouted as he leaped for Dom Vincente. Steel flashed in the moonlight and the Spaniard's sword was through Carlos ere he could move.

And the shadows rose about us. Then it was back to back, sword and dagger, three men against a hundred. Spears flashed, and a fiendish yell went up from savage throats. I spitted three natives in as many thrusts and then went down from a stunning swing from a war-club, and an instant later Dom Vincente fell upon me, with a spear in one arm and another through the leg. Don Florenzo was standing above us, sword leaping like a live thing, when a charge of the arquebusiers swept the river bank clear and we were borne into the castle.

The black hordes came with a rush, spears flashing like a wave of steel, a thunderous roar of savagery going up to the skies.

Time and again they swept up the slopes, bounding the moat, until they were swarming over the palisades. And time and again the fire of the hundred-odd defenders hurled them back.

They had set fire to the plundered warehouses, and their light vied with the light of the moon. Just across the river there was a larger storehouse, and about this hordes of the natives gathered, tearing it apart for plunder.

"Would that they would drop a torch upon it," said Dom Vincente, "for naught is stored therein save some thousand pounds of gunpowder. I dared not store the treacherous stuff this side of the river. All the tribes of the river and coast have gathered for our slaughter and all my ships are upon the seas. We may hold out awhile, but eventually they will swarm the palisade and put us to the slaughter."

I hastened to the dungeon wherein de Montour sat. Outside the door I called to him and he bade me enter in voice which told me the fiend had left him for an instant.

"The blacks have risen," I told him.

"I guessed as much. How goes the battle?"

I gave him the details of the betrayal and the fight, and mentioned the powder-house across the river. He sprang to his feet.

"Now by my hag-ridden soul!" he exclaimed. "I will fling the dice once more with Hell! Swift, let me out of the castle! I will essay to swim the river and set off yon powder!"

"It is insanity!" I exclaimed. "A thousand blacks lurk between the palisades and the river, and thrice that number beyond! The river itself swarms with crocodiles!"

"I will attempt it!" he answered, a great light in his face. "If I can reach it, some thousand natives will lighten the siege; if I am slain, then my soul is free and mayhap will gain some forgiveness for that I gave my life to atone for my crimes."

Then, "Haste," he exclaimed, "for the demon is returning! Already I feel his influence! Haste ye!"

For the castle gates we sped, and as de Montour ran he gasped as a man in a terrific battle.

At the gate he pitched headlong, then rose, to spring through it. Wild yells greeted him from the natives.

The arquebusiers shouted curses at him and at me. Peering down from the top of the palisades I saw him turn from side to side uncertainly. A score of natives were rushing recklessly forward, spears raised.

Then the eerie wolf-yell rose to the skies, and de Montour bounded forward. Aghast, the natives paused, and before a man of them could move he was among them. Wild shrieks, not of rage, but of terror.

In amazement the arquebusiers held their fire.

Straight through the group of blacks de Montour charged, and when they broke and fled, three of them fled not.

A dozen steps de Montour took in pursuit; then stopped stock-still. A moment he stood so, while spears flew about him, then turned and ran swiftly in the direction of the river.

A few steps from the river another band of blacks barred his way. In the flaming light of the burning houses the scene was clearly illuminated. A thrown spear tore through de Montour's shoulder. Without pausing in his stride he tore it forth and drove it through a native, leaping over his body to get among the others.

They could not face the fiend-driven white man. With shrieks they fled, and de Montour, bounding upon the back of one, brought him down.

Then he rose, staggered and sprang to the river bank. An instant he paused there and then vanished in the shadows.

"Name of the devil!" gasped Dom Vincente at my shoulder. "What manner of man is that? Was that de Montour?"

I nodded. The wild yells of the natives rose above the crackle of the arquebusiers' fire. They were massed thick about the great warehouse across the river.

"They plan a great rush," said Dom Vincente. "They will swarm clear over the palisade, methinks. Ha!"

A crash that seemed to rip the skies apart! A burst of flame that mounted to the stars! The castle rocked with the explosion. Then silence, as the smoke, drifting away, showed only a great crater where the warehouse had stood.

I could tell of how Dom Vincente led a charge, crippled as he was, out of the castle gate and down the slope, to fall upon the terrified blacks who had escaped the explosion. I could tell of the slaughter, of the victory and the pursuit of the fleeing natives.

I could tell, too, *Messieurs,* of how I became separated from the band and of how I wandered far into the jungle, unable to find my way back to the coast.

I could tell how I was captured by a wandering band of slave raiders, and of how I escaped. But such is not my intention. In itself it would make a long tale; and it is of de Montour that I am speaking.

I thought much of the things that had passed and wondered if indeed de Montour reached the storehouse to blow it to the skies or whether it was but the deed of chance.

That a man could swim that reptile-swarming river, fiend-driven though he was, seemed impossible. And if he blew up the storehouse, he must have gone up with it.

So one night I pushed my way wearily through the jungle and sighted the coast, and close to the shore a small, tumble-down hut of thatch. To it I went, thinking to sleep therein if insects and reptiles would allow.

I entered the doorway and then stopped short. Upon a makeshift stool sat a man. He looked up as I entered and the rays of the moon fell across his face.

I started back with a ghastly thrill of horror. *It was de Montour, and the moon was full!*

Then as I stood, unable to flee, he rose and came toward me. And his face, though haggard as of a man who has looked into Hell, was the face of a sane man.

"Come in, my friend," he said, and there was a great peace in his voice. "Come in and fear me not. The fiend has left me forever."

"But tell me, how conquered you?" I exclaimed as I grasped his hand.

"I fought a frightful battle, as I ran to the river," he answered, "for the fiend had me in its grasp and drove me to fall upon the natives. But for the first time my soul and mind gained ascendancy for an instant, an instant just long enough to hold me to my purpose. And I believe the good saints came to my aid, for I was giving my life to save life.

"I leaped into the river and swam, and in an instant the crocodiles were swarming about me.

"Again in the clutch of the fiend I fought them, there in the river. Then suddenly the *thing* left me.

"I climbed from the river and fired the warehouse. The explosion hurled me hundreds of feet, and for days I wandered witless through the jungle.

"But the full moon came, and came again, and I felt not the influence of the fiend.

"I am free, free!" And a wondrous note of exultation, nay, *exaltation,* thrilled his words:

"My soul is free. Incredible as it seems, the demon lies drowned upon the bed of the river, or else inhabits the body of one of the savage reptiles that swim the ways of the Niger."

THE LOST RACE

Weird Tales, January 1927

Cororuc glanced about him and hastened his pace. He was no coward, but he did not like the place. Tall trees rose all about, their sullen branches shutting out the sunlight. The dim trail led in and out among them, sometimes skirting the edge of a ravine, where Cororuc could gaze down at the treetops beneath. Occasionally, through a rift in the forest, he could see away to the forbidding hills that hinted of the ranges much farther to the west, that were the mountains of Cornwall.

In those mountains the bandit chief, Buruc the Cruel, was supposed to lurk, to descend upon such victims as might pass that way. Cororuc shifted his grip on his spear and quickened his step. His haste was due not only to the menace of the outlaws, but also to the fact that he wished once more to be in his native land. He had been on a secret mission to the wild Cornish tribesmen; and though he had been more or less successful, he was impatient to be out of their inhospitable country. It had been a long, wearisome trip, and he still had nearly the whole of Britain to traverse. He threw a glance of aversion about him. He longed for the pleasant woodlands, with scampering deer, and chirping birds, to which he was used. He longed for the tall white cliff, where the blue sea lapped merrily. The forest through which he was passing seemed uninhabited. There were no birds, no animals; nor had he seen a sign of human habitation.

His comrades still lingered at the savage court of the Cornish king, enjoying his crude hospitality, in no hurry to be away. But Cororuc was not content. So he had left them to follow at their leisure and had set out alone.

Rather a fine figure of a man was Cororuc. Some six feet in height, strongly though leanly built, he was, with gray eyes, a pure Briton but not a pure Celt, his long yellow hair revealing, in him as in all his race, a trace of Belgae.

He was clad in skillfully dressed deerskin, for the Celts had not yet perfected the coarse cloth which they made, and most of the race preferred the hides of deer.

He was armed with a long bow of yew wood, made with no especial skill but an efficient weapon; a long bronze broadsword, with a buckskin sheath; a long bronze dagger and a small, round shield, rimmed with a band of bronze and covered with tough buffalo hide. A crude bronze helmet was on his head. Faint devices were painted in woad on his arms and cheeks.

His beardless face was of the highest type of Briton, clear, straightforward, the shrewd, practical determination of the Nordic mingling with the reckless courage and dreamy artistry of the Celt.

So Cororuc trod the forest path, warily, ready to flee or fight, but preferring to do neither just then.

The trail led away from the ravine, disappearing around a great tree. And from the other side of the tree, Cororuc heard sounds of conflict. Gliding warily forward, and wondering whether he should see some of the elves and dwarfs that were reputed to haunt those woodlands, he peered around the great tree.

A few feet from him he saw a strange tableau. Backed against another tree stood a large wolf, at bay, blood trickling from gashes about his shoulder; while before him, crouching for a spring, the warrior saw a great panther. Cororuc wondered at the cause of the battle. Not often the lords of the forest met in warfare. And he was puzzled by the snarls of the great cat. Savage, blood-lusting, yet they held a strange note of fear; and the beast seemed hesitant to spring in.

Just why Cororuc chose to take the part of the wolf, he himself could not have said. Doubtless it was just the reckless chivalry of the Celt in him, an admiration for the dauntless attitude of the wolf against his far more powerful foe. Be that as it may, Cororuc, characteristically forgetting his bow and taking the more reckless course, drew his sword and leaped in front of the panther. But he had no chance to use it. The panther, whose nerve appeared to be already somewhat shaken, uttered a startled screech and disappeared among the trees so quickly that Cororuc wondered if he had really seen a panther. He turned to the wolf, wondering if it would leap upon him. It was watching him, half crouching; slowly it stepped away from the tree, and still watching him, backed away a few yards, then turned and made off with a strange shambling gait. As the warrior watched it vanish into the forest, an uncanny feeling came over him; he had seen many wolves, he had hunted them and had been hunted by them, but he had never seen such a wolf before.

He hesitated and then walked warily after the wolf, following the tracks that were plainly defined in the soft loam. He did not hasten, being merely content to follow the tracks. After a short distance, he stopped short, the hairs on his neck seeming to bristle. *Only the tracks of the hind feet showed: the wolf was walking erect.*

He glanced about him. There was no sound; the forest was silent. He felt an impulse to turn and put as much territory between him and the mystery as possible, but his Celtic curiosity would not allow it. He followed the trail. And then it ceased altogether. Beneath a great tree the tracks vanished. Cororuc felt the cold sweat on his forehead. What kind of place was that forest? Was he being led astray and eluded by some inhuman, supernatural monster of the woodlands, who sought to ensnare him? And Cororuc backed away, his sword lifted, his courage not allowing him to run, but greatly desiring to do so. And so he came again to the tree where he had first seen the wolf. The trail he had followed led away from it in another direction and Cororuc took it up, almost running in his haste to get out of the vicinity of a wolf who walked on two legs and then vanished in the air.

The trail wound about more tediously than ever, appearing and disappearing within a dozen feet, but it was well for Cororuc that it did, for thus he heard the voices of the men coming up the path before they saw him. He took to a tall tree that branched over the trail, lying close to the great bole, along a wide-flung branch.

Three men were coming down the forest path.

One was a big, burly fellow, vastly over six feet in height, with a long red beard and a great mop of red hair. In contrast, his eyes were a beady black. He was dressed in deerskins, and armed with a great sword.

Of the two others, one was a lanky, villainous-looking scoundrel, with only one eye, and the other was a small, wizened man, who squinted hideously with both beady eyes.

Cororuc knew them, by descriptions the Cornishmen had made between curses, and it was in his excitement to get a better view of the most villainous murderer in Britain that he slipped from the tree branch and plunged to the ground directly between them.

He was up on the instant, his sword out. He could expect no mercy; for he knew that the red-haired man was Buruc the Cruel, the scourge of Cornwall.

The bandit chief bellowed a foul curse and whipped out his great sword. He avoided the Briton's furious thrust by a swift backward leap and then the battle was on. Buruc rushed the warrior from the front, striving to beat him down by sheer weight; while the lanky, one-eyed villain slipped around, trying to get behind him. The smaller man had retreated to the edge of the forest. The fine art of the fence was unknown to those early swordsmen. It was hack, slash, stab, the full weight of the arm behind each blow. The terrific blows crashing on his shield beat Cororuc to the ground, and the lanky, one-eyed villain rushed in to finish him. Cororuc spun about without rising, cut the bandit's legs from under him and stabbed him as he fell, then threw himself to one side and to his feet, in time to avoid Buruc's sword. Again, driving his shield up to catch the bandit's sword in midair, he deflected it and whirled his own with all his power. Buruc's head flew from his shoulders.

Then Cororuc, turning, saw the wizened bandit scurry into the forest. He raced after him, but the fellow had disappeared among the trees. Knowing the uselessness of attempting to pursue him, Cororuc turned and raced down the trail. He did not know if there were more bandits in that direction, but he did know that if he expected to get out of the forest at all, he would have to do it swiftly. Without doubt the villain who had escaped would have all the other bandits out, and soon they would be beating the woodlands for him.

After running for some distance down the path and seeing no sign of any enemy, he stopped and climbed into the topmost branches of a tall tree that towered above its fellows.

On all sides he seemed surrounded by a leafy ocean. To the west he could see the hills he had avoided. To the north, far in the distance, other hills rose; to the south the forest ran, an unbroken sea. But to the east, far away, he could barely see the line that marked the thinning out of the forest into the fertile plains. Miles and miles away, he knew not how many, but it meant more pleasant travel, villages of men, people of his own race. He was surprized that he was able to see that far, but the tree in which he stood was a giant of its kind.

Before he started to descend, he glanced about nearer at hand. He could trace the faintly marked line of the trail he had been following, running away into the east; and could make out other trails leading into it, or away from it. Then a glint caught his eye. He fixed his gaze on a glade some distance down the trail and saw, presently, a party of men enter and vanish. Here and there, on every trail, he caught glances of the glint of accouterments, the waving of foliage. So the squinting villain had already roused the bandits. They were all around him; he was virtually surrounded.

A faintly heard burst of savage yells, from back up the trail, startled him. So, they had already thrown a cordon about the place of the fight and had found him gone. Had he not fled swiftly, he would have been caught. He was outside the cordon, but the bandits were all about him. Swiftly he slipped from the tree and glided into the forest.

Then began the most exciting hunt Cororuc had ever engaged in; for he was the hunted and men were the hunters. Gliding, slipping from bush to bush and from tree to tree, now running swiftly, now crouching in a covert, Cororuc fled, ever eastward, not daring to turn back lest he be driven farther back into the forest. At times he was forced to turn his course; in fact, he very seldom fled in a straight course, yet always he managed to work farther eastward.

Sometimes he crouched in bushes or lay along some leafy branch, and saw bandits pass so close to him that he could have touched them. Once or twice they sighted him and he fled, bounding over logs and bushes, darting in and out among the trees; and always he eluded them.

It was in one of those headlong flights that he noticed he had entered a defile of small hills, of which he had been unaware, and looking back over his shoulder, saw that his pursuers had halted, within full sight. Without pausing to ruminate on so strange a thing, he darted around a great boulder, felt a vine or something catch his foot, and was thrown headlong. Simultaneously, something struck the youth's head, knocking him senseless.

When Cororuc recovered his senses, he found that he was bound, hand and foot. He was being borne along, over rough ground. He looked about him. Men carried him on their shoulders, but such men as he had never seen before. Scarce above four feet stood the tallest, and they were small of build and very dark of complexion. Their eyes were black; and most of them went stooped forward, as if from a lifetime spent in crouching and hiding; peering furtively on all sides. They were armed with small bows, arrows, spears and daggers, all pointed, not with crudely worked bronze but with flint and obsidian, of the finest workmanship. They were dressed in finely dressed hides of rabbits and other small animals, and a kind of coarse cloth; and many were tattooed from head to foot in ocher and woad. There were perhaps twenty in all. What sort of men were they? Cororuc had never seen the like.

They were going down a ravine, on both sides of which steep cliffs rose. Presently they seemed to come to a blank wall, where the ravine appeared to come to an abrupt stop. Here, at a word from one who seemed to be in command, they set the Briton down, and seizing hold of a large boulder, drew it to one side. A small cavern was exposed, seeming to vanish away into the earth; then the strange men picked up the Briton and moved forward.

Cororuc's hair bristled at the thought of being borne into that forbidding-looking cave. What manner of men were they? In all Britain and Alba, in Cornwall or Ireland, Cororuc had never seen such men. Small dwarfish men, who dwelt in the earth. Cold sweat broke out on the youth's forehead. Surely they were the malevolent dwarfs of whom the Cornish people had spoken, who dwelt in their caverns by day, and by night sallied forth to steal and burn dwellings, even slaying if the opportunity arose! You will hear of them, even today, if you journey in Cornwall.

The men, or elves, if such they were, bore him into the cavern, others entering and drawing the boulder back into place. For a moment all was darkness, and then torches began to glow, away off. And at a shout they moved on. Other men of the caves came forward, with the torches.

Cororuc looked about him. The torches shed a vague glow over the scene. Sometimes one, sometimes another wall of the cave showed for an instant, and the Briton was vaguely aware that they were covered with paintings, crudely done, yet with a certain skill his own race could not equal. But always the roof remained unseen. Cororuc knew that the seemingly small cavern had merged into a cave of surprizing size. Through the vague light of the torches the strange people moved, came and went, silently, like shadows of the dim past.

He felt the cords of thongs that bound his feet loosened. He was lifted upright.

"Walk straight ahead," said a voice, speaking the language of his own race, and he felt a spear point touch the back of his neck.

And straight ahead he walked, feeling his sandals scrape on the stone floor of the cave, until they came to a place where the floor tilted upward. The pitch was steep and the stone was so slippery that Cororuc could not have climbed it alone. But his captors pushed him, and pulled him, and he saw that long, strong vines were strung from somewhere at the top.

Those the strange men seized, and bracing their feet against the slippery ascent, went up swiftly. When their feet found level surface again, the cave made a turn, and Cororuc blundered out into a fire-lit scene that made him gasp.

The cave debouched into a cavern so vast as to be almost incredible. The mighty walls swept up into a great arched roof that vanished in the darkness. A level floor lay between, and through it flowed a river; an underground river. From under one wall it flowed to vanish silently under the other. An arched stone bridge, seemingly of natural make, spanned the current.

All around the walls of the great cavern, which was roughly circular, were smaller caves, and before each glowed a fire. Higher up were other caves, regularly arranged, tier on tier. Surely human men could not have built such a city.

In and out among the caves, on the level floor of the main cavern, people were going about what seemed daily tasks. Men were talking together and mending weapons, some were fishing from the river; women were replenishing fires, preparing garments; and altogether it might have been any other village in Britain, to judge from their occupations. But it all struck Cororuc as extremely unreal; the strange place, the small, silent people, going about their tasks, the river flowing silently through it all.

Then they became aware of the prisoner and flocked about him. There was none of the shouting, abuse and indignities, such as savages usually heap on their captives, as the small men drew about Cororuc, silently eying him with malevolent, wolfish stares. The warrior shuddered, in spite of himself.

But his captors pushed through the throng, driving the Briton before them. Close to the bank of the river, they stopped and drew away from around him.

Two great fires leaped and flickered in front of him and there was something between them. He focused his gaze and presently made out the object. A high stone seat, like a throne; and in it seated an aged man, with a long white beard, silent, motionless, but with black eyes that gleamed like a wolf's.

The ancient was clothed in some kind of a single, flowing garment. One claw-like hand rested on the seat near him, skinny, crooked fingers, with talons like a hawk's. The other hand was hidden among his garments.

The firelight danced and flickered; now the old man stood out clearly, his hooked, beak-like nose and long beard thrown into bold relief; now he seemed to recede until he was invisible to the gaze of the Briton, except for his glittering eyes.

"Speak, Briton!" The words came suddenly, strong, clear, without a hint of age. "Speak, what would ye say?"

Cororuc, taken aback, stammered and said, "Why, why — what manner people are you? Why have you taken me prisoner? Are you elves?"

"We are Picts," was the stern reply.

"Picts!" Cororuc had heard tales of those ancient people from the Gaelic Britons; some said that they still lurked in the hills of Siluria, but —

"I have fought Picts in Caledonia," the Briton protested; "they are short but massive and misshapen; not at all like you!"

"They are not true Picts," came the stern retort. "Look about you, Briton," with a wave of an arm, "you see the remnants of a vanishing race; a race that once ruled Britain from sea to sea."

The Briton stared, bewildered.

"Harken, Briton," the voice continued; "harken, barbarian, while I tell to you the tale of the lost race."

The firelight flickered and danced, throwing vague reflections on the towering walls and on the rushing, silent current.

The ancient's voice echoed through the mighty cavern.

"Our people came from the south. Over the islands, over the Inland Sea. Over the snow-topped mountains, where some remained, to slay any enemies who might follow. Down into the fertile plains we came. Over all the land we spread. We became wealthy and prosperous. Then two kings arose in the land, and he who conquered, drove out the conquered. So many of us made boats and set sail for the far-off cliffs that gleamed white in the sunlight. We found a fair land with fertile plains. We found a race of red-haired barbarians, who dwelt in caves. Mighty giants, of great bodies and small minds.

"We built our huts of wattle. We tilled the soil. We cleared the forest. We drove the red-haired giants back into the forest. Farther we drove them back until at last they fled to the mountains of the west and the mountains of the north. We were rich. We were prosperous.

"Then," and his voice thrilled with rage and hate, until it seemed to reverberate through the cavern, "then the Celts came. From the isles of the west, in their rude coracles they came. In the west they landed, but they were not satisfied with the west. They marched eastward and seized the fertile plains. We fought. They were stronger. They were fierce fighters and they were armed with weapons of bronze, whereas we had only weapons of flint.

"We were driven out. They enslaved us. They drove us into the forest. Some of us fled into the mountains of the west. Many fled into the mountains of the north. There they mingled with the red-haired giants we drove out so long ago, and became a race of monstrous dwarfs, losing all the arts of peace and gaining only the ability to fight.

"But some of us swore that we would never leave the land we had fought for. But the Celts pressed us. There were many, and more came. So we took to caverns, to ravines, to caves. We, who had always dwelt in huts that let in much light, who had always tilled the soil, we learned to dwell like beasts, in caves where no sunlight ever entered. Caves we found, of which this is the greatest; caves we made.

"You, Briton," the voice became a shriek and a long arm was outstretched in accusation, "you and your race! You have made a free, prosperous nation into a race of earth-rats! We who never fled, who dwelt in the air and the sunlight close by the sea where traders came, we must flee like hunted beasts and burrow like moles! But at night! Ah, then for our vengeance! Then we slip from our hiding places, ravines and caves, with torch and dagger! Look, Briton!"

And following the gesture, Cororuc saw a rounded post of some kind of very hard wood, set in a niche in the stone floor, close to the bank. The floor about the niche was charred as if by old fires.

Cororuc stared, uncomprehending. Indeed, he understood little of what had passed. That these people were even human, he was not at all certain. He had heard so much of them as "little people." Tales of their doings, their hatred of the race of man, and their maliciousness flocked back to him. Little he knew that he was gazing on one of the mysteries of the ages. That the tales which the ancient Gaels told of the Picts, already warped, would become even more warped from age to age, to result in tales of elves, dwarfs, trolls and fairies, at first accepted and then rejected, entire, by the race of men, just as the Neanderthal monsters resulted in tales of goblins and ogres. But of that Cororuc neither knew nor cared, and the ancient was speaking again.

"There, there, Briton," exulted he, pointing to the post, "there you shall pay! A scant payment for the debt your race owes mine, but to the fullest of your extent."

The old man's exultation would have been fiendish, except for a certain high purpose in his face. He was sincere. He believed that he was only taking just vengeance; and he seemed like some great patriot for a mighty, lost cause.

"But I am a Briton!" stammered Cororuc. "It was not my people who drove your race into exile! They were Gaels, from Ireland. I am a Briton and my race came from Gallia only a hundred years ago. We conquered the Gaels and drove them into Erin, Wales and Caledonia, even as they drove your race."

"No matter!" The ancient chief was on his feet. "A Celt is a Celt. Briton, or Gael, it makes no difference. Had it not been Gael, it would have been Briton. Every Celt who falls into our hands must pay, be it warrior or woman, babe or king. Seize him and bind him to the post."

In an instant Cororuc was bound to the post, and he saw, with horror, the Picts piling firewood about his feet.

"And when you are sufficiently burned, Briton," said the ancient, "this dagger that has drunk the blood of a hundred Britons, shall quench its thirst in yours."

"But never have I harmed a Pict!" Cororuc gasped, struggling with his bonds.

"You pay, not for what you did, but for what your race has done," answered the ancient sternly. "Well do I remember the deeds of the Celts when first they landed on Britain — the shrieks of the slaughtered, the screams of ravished girls, the smokes of burning villages, the plundering."

Cororuc felt his short neck-hairs bristle. When first the Celts landed on Britain! That was over five hundred years ago!

And his Celtic curiosity would not let him keep still, even at the stake with the Picts preparing to light firewood piled about him.

"You could not remember that. That was ages ago."

The ancient looked at him somberly. "And I am age-old. In my youth I was a witch-finder, and an old woman witch cursed me as she writhed at the stake. She said I should live until the last child of the Pictish race had passed. That I should see the once mighty nation go down into oblivion and then — and only then — should I follow it. For she put upon me the curse of life everlasting."

Then his voice rose until it filled the cavern. "But the curse was nothing. Words can do no harm, can do nothing, to a man. I live. A hundred generations have I seen come and go, and yet another hundred. What is time? The sun rises and sets, and another day has passed into oblivion. Men watch the sun and set their lives by it. They league themselves on every hand with time. They count the minutes that race them into eternity. Man outlived the centuries ere he began to reckon time. Time is man-made. Eternity is the work of the gods. In this cavern there is no such thing as time. There are no stars, no sun. Without is time; within is eternity. We count not time. Nothing marks the speeding of the hours. The youths go forth. They see the sun, the stars. They reckon time. And they pass. I was a young man when I entered this cavern. I have never left it. As you reckon time, I may have dwelt here a thousand years; or an hour. When not banded by time, the soul, the mind, call it what you will, can conquer the body. And the wise men of the race, in my youth, knew more than the outer world will ever learn. When I feel that my body begins to weaken, I take the magic draft, that is known only to me, of all the world. It does not give immortality; that is the work of the mind alone; but it rebuilds the body. The race of Picts vanish; they fade like the snow on the mountain. And when the last is gone, this dagger shall free me from the world." Then in a swift change of tone, "Light the fagots!"

Cororuc's mind was fairly reeling. He did not in the least understand what he had just heard. He was positive that he was going mad; and what he saw the next minute assured him of it.

Through the throng came a wolf; and he knew that it was the wolf whom he had rescued from the panther close by the ravine in the forest!

Strange, how long ago and far away that seemed! Yes, it was the same wolf. That same strange, shambling gait. Then the thing stood erect and raised its front feet to its head. What nameless horror was that?

Then the wolf's head fell back, disclosing a man's face. The face of a Pict; one of the first "werewolves." The man stepped out of the wolfskin and strode forward, calling something. A Pict just starting to light the wood about the Briton's feet drew back the torch and hesitated.

The wolf-Pict stepped forward and began to speak to the chief, using Celtic, evidently for the prisoner's benefit. Cororuc was surprized to hear so many speak his language, not reflecting upon its comparative simplicity, and the ability of the Picts.

"What is this?" asked the Pict who had played wolf. "A man is to be burned who should not be!"

"How?" exclaimed the old man fiercely, clutching his long beard. "Who are you to go against a custom of age-old antiquity?"

"I met a panther," answered the other, "and this Briton risked his life to save mine. Shall a Pict show ingratitude?"

And as the ancient hesitated, evidently pulled one way by his fanatical lust for revenge, and the other by his equally fierce racial pride, the Pict burst into a wild flight of oration, carried on in his own language. At last the ancient chief nodded.

"A Pict ever paid his debts," said he with impressive grandeur. "Never a Pict forgets. Unbind him. No Celt shall ever say that a Pict showed ingratitude."

Cororuc was released, and as, like a man in a daze, he tried to stammer his thanks, the chief waved them aside.

"A Pict never forgets a foe, ever remembers a friendly deed," he replied.

"Come," murmured his Pictish friend, tugging at the Celt's arm.

He led the way into a cave leading away from the main cavern. As they went, Cororuc looked back, to see the ancient chief seated upon his stone throne, his eyes gleaming as he seemed to gaze back through the lost glories of the ages; on each hand the fires leaped and flickered. A figure of grandeur, the king of a lost race.

On and on Cororuc's guide led him. And at last they emerged and the Briton saw the starlit sky above him.

"In that way is a village of your tribesmen," said the Pict, pointing, "where you will find a welcome until you wish to take up your journey anew."

And he pressed gifts on the Celt; gifts of garments of cloth and finely worked deerskin, beaded belts, a fine horn bow with arrows skillfully tipped with obsidian. Gifts of food. His own weapons were returned to him.

"But an instant," said the Briton, as the Pict turned to go. "I followed your tracks in the forest. They vanished." There was a question in his voice.

The Pict laughed softly. "I leaped into the branches of the tree. Had you looked up, you would have seen me. If ever you wish a friend, you will ever find one in Berula, chief among the Alban Picts."

He turned and vanished. And Cororuc strode through the moonlight toward the Celtic village.

THE SONG OF THE BATS

Weird Tales, May 1927

The dusk was on the mountain
And the stars were dim and frail
When the bats came flying, flying
From the river and the vale
To wheel against the twilight
And sing their witchy tale.

"We were kings of eld!" they chanted,
"Rulers of a world enchanted;
"Every nation of creation
"Owned our lordship over men.
"Diadems of power crowned us,
"Then rose Solomon to confound us,
"Flung his web of magic round us,
"In the forms of beasts he bound us,
"So our rule was broken then."

Whirling, wheeling into westward,
Fled they in their phantom flight;
Was it but a wing-beat music
Murmured through the star-gemmed night?
Or the singing of a ghost clan
Whispering of forgotten night?

THE RIDE OF FALUME

Weird Tales, October 1927

Falume of Spain rode forth amain when twilight's crimson fell
To drink a toast with Bahram's ghost in the scarlet land of Hell.
His rowels clashed as swift he dashed along the flaming skies;
The sunset rade at his bridle braid and the moon was in his eyes.
The waves were green with an eery sheen over the hills of Thule
And the ripples beat to his horse's feet like a serpent in a pool.
On vampire wings the shadow things wheeled round and
round his head,
Till he came at last to a kingdom vast in the Land of the Restless Dead.

They thronged about in a grisly rout, they caught at his silver rein;
"Avaunt, foul host! Tell Bahram's ghost Falume has come from Spain!"
Then flame-arrayed rose Bahram's shade: "What would ye
have, Falume?"
"Ho, Bahram who on earth I slew where Tagus' waters boom,
Now though I shore your life of yore amid the burning West,
I ride to Hell to bid ye tell where I might ride to rest.
My beard is white and dim my sight and I would fain be gone.
Speak without guile: where lies the isle of mystic Avalon?"

"A league beyond the western wind, a mile beyond the moon,
Where the dim seas roar on an unknown shore and the drifting
stars lie strewn:
The lotus buds there scent the woods where the quiet rivers gleam,
And king and knight in the mystic light the ages drowse and dream."
With sudden bound Falume wheeled round, he fled through
the flying wrack
Till he came to the land of Spain with the sunset at his back.
"No dreams for me, but living free, red wine and battle's roar;
I breast the gales and I ride the trails until I ride no more."

THE RIDERS OF BABYLON

Weird Tales, January 1928

The riders of Babylon clatter forth
Like the hawk-winged scourgers of Azrael
To the meadow-lands of the South and North
And the strong-walled cities of Israel.
They harry the men of the caravans,
They bring rare plunder across the sands
To deck the throne of the great god Baal.
But Babylon's king is a broken shell
And Babylon's queen is a sprite from Hell;
And men shall say, "Here Babylon fell,"
Ere Time has forgot the tale.

The riders of Babylon come and go
From Gaza's halls to the shores of Tyre;
They shake the world from the lands of snow
To the deserts, red in the sunset's fire;
Their horses swim in a sea of gore
And the tribes of the earth bow down before;
They have chained the seas where the Cretans sail.
But Babylon's sun shall set in blood;
Her towers shall sink in a crimson flood;
And men shall say, "Here Babylon stood,"
Ere Time forgot the tale.

THE DREAM SNAKE

Weird Tales, February 1928

The night was strangely still. As we sat upon the wide veranda, gazing out over the broad, shadowy lawns, the silence of the hour entered our spirits and for a long while no one spoke.

Then far across the dim mountains that fringed the eastern skyline, a faint haze began to glow, and presently a great golden moon came up, making a ghostly radiance over the land and etching boldly the dark clumps of shadows that were trees. A light breeze came whispering out of the east, and the unmowed grass swayed before it in long, sinuous waves, dimly visible in the moonlight; and from among the group upon the veranda there came a swift gasp, a sharp intake of breath that caused us all to turn and gaze.

Faming was leaning forward, clutching the arms of his chair, his face strange and pallid in the spectral light; a thin trickle of blood seeping from the lip in which he had set his teeth. Amazed, we looked at him, and suddenly he jerked about with a short, snarling laugh.

"There's no need of gawking at me like a flock of sheep!" he said irritably and stopped short. We sat bewildered, scarcely knowing what sort of reply to make, and suddenly he burst out again.

"Now I guess I'd better tell the whole thing or you'll be going off and putting me down as a lunatic. Don't interrupt me, any of you! I want to get this thing off my mind. You all know that I'm not a very imaginative man; but there's a thing, purely a figment of imagination, that has haunted me since babyhood. A dream!" he fairly cringed back in his chair as he muttered, "A dream! And God, what a dream! The first time — no, I can't remember the first time I ever dreamed it — I've been dreaming the hellish thing ever since I can remember. Now it's this way: there is a sort of bungalow, set upon a hill in the midst of wide grasslands — not unlike this estate; but this scene is in Africa. And I am living there with a sort of servant, a Hindoo. Just why I am there is never clear to my waking mind, though I am always aware of the reason in my dreams. As a man of a dream, I remember my past life (a life which in no way corresponds with my waking life), but when I am awake my subconscious mind fails to transmit these impressions. However, I think that I am a fugitive from justice and the Hindoo is also a fugitive. How the bungalow came to be there I can never remember, nor do I know in what part of Africa it is, though all these things are known to my dream self. But the bungalow is a small one of a very few rooms, and it situated upon the top of the hill, as I said There are no other hills about and the grasslands stretch to the horizon in every direction; knee-high in some places, waist-high in others.

"Now the dream always opens as I am coming up the hill, just as the sun is beginning to set. I am carrying a broken rifle and I have been on a hunting trip; how the rifle was broken, and the full details of the trip, I clearly remember — dreaming. But never upon waking. It is just as if a curtain were suddenly raised and a drama began; or just as if I were suddenly transferred to another man's body and life, remembering past years of that life, and not cognizant of any other existence. And that is the hellish part of it! As you know, most of us, dreaming, are, at the back of our consciousness, aware that we are dreaming. No matter how horrible the dream may become, we know that it is a dream, and thus insanity or possible death is staved off. But in this particular dream, there is no such knowledge. I tell you it is so vivid, so complete in every detail, that I wonder sometimes if that is not my real existence and this a dream! But no; for then I should have been dead years ago.

"As I was saying, I come up the hill and the first thing I am cognizant of that it is out of the ordinary is a sort of track leading up the hill in an irregular way; that is, the grass is mashed down as if something heavy had been dragged over it. But I pay no especial attention to it, for I am thinking, with some irritation, that the broken rifle I carry is my only arm and that now I must forego hunting until I can send for another.

"You see, I remember thoughts and impressions of the dream itself, of the occurrences of the dream; it is the memories that the dream 'I' had, of that other dream existence that I can not remember. So. I come up the hill and enter the bungalow. The doors are open and the Hindoo is not there. But the main room is in confusion; chairs are broken, a table is overturned. The Hindoo's dagger is lying upon the floor, but there is no blood anywhere.

"Now, in my dreams, I never remember the other dreams, as sometimes one does. Always it is the first dream, the first time. I always experience the same sensations, in my dreams, with as vivid a force as the first time I ever dreamed. So. I am not able to understand this. The Hindoo is gone, but (thus I ruminate, standing in the center of the disordered room) what did away with him? Had it been a raiding party of Negroes they would have looted the bungalow and probably burned it. Had it been a lion, the place would have been smeared with blood. Then suddenly I remember the track I saw going up the hill, and a cold hand touches my spine; for instantly the whole thing is clear: the thing that came up from the grasslands and wrought havoc in the little bungalow could be naught else except a giant serpent. And as I think or the size of the spoor, cold sweat beads my forehead and the broken rifle shakes in my hand.

"Then I rush to the door in a wild panic, my only thought to make a dash for the coast. But the sun has set and dusk is stealing across the grasslands. And out there somewhere, lurking in the tall grass is that grisly thing — that horror. God!" The ejaculation broke from his lips with such feeling that all of us started, not realizing the tension we had reached. There was a second's silence, then he continued:

"So I bolt the doors and windows, light the lamp I have and take my stand in the middle of the room. And I stand like a statue — waiting — listening. After a while the moon comes up and her haggard light drifts though the windows. And I stand still in the center of the room; the night is very still — something like this night; the breeze occasionally whispers through the grass, and each time I start and clench my hands until the nails bite into the flesh and the blood trickles down my wrists — and I stand there and wait and listen but it does not come that night!" The sentence came suddenly and explosively, and an involuntary sigh came from the rest; a relaxing of tension.

"I am determined, if I live the night through, to start for the coast early the next morning, taking my chance out there in the grim grasslands — with it. But with morning, I dare not. I do not know in which direction the monster went; and I dare not risk coming upon him in the open, unarmed as I am. So, as in a maze, I remain at the bungalow, and ever my eyes turn toward the sun, lurching relentless down the sky toward the horizon. Ah, God! if I could but halt the sun in the sky!"

The man was in the clutch of some terrific power; his words fairly leaped at us.

"Then the sun rocks down the sky and the long gray shadows

come stalking across the grasslands. Dizzy with fear, I have bolted the doors and windows and lighted the lamp long before the last faint glow of twilight fades. The light from the windows may attract the monster, but I dare not stay in the dark. And again I take my stand in the center of the room — waiting."

There was a shuddersome halt. Then he continued, barely above a whisper, moistening his lips: "'There is no knowing how long I stand there; Time has ceased to be and each second is an eon; each minute is an eternity, stretching into endless eternities. Then, God! but what is that?" He leaned forward, the moonlight etching his face into such a mask of horrified listening that each of us shivered and flung a hasty glance over our shoulders.

"Not the night breeze this time," he whispered. "Something makes the grasses swish-swish — as if a great, long, plaint weight were being dragged through them. Above the bungalow it swishes and then ceases — in front of the door; then the hinges creak — creak! The door begins to bulge inward — a small bit — then some more!" The man's arms were held in front of him, as if braced strongly against something, and his breath came in quick gasps. "And I know I should lean against the door and hold it shut, but I do not, I can not move. I stand there, like a sheep waiting to be slaughtered — but the door holds!" Again that sigh expressive of pent-up feeling.

He drew a shaky hand across his brow. "And all night I stand in the center of that room, as motionless as an image, except to turn slowly, as the swish-swish of the grass marks the fiend's course about the house. Ever I keep my eyes in the direction of the soft, sinister sound. Sometimes it ceases for an instant, or for several minutes, and then I stand scarcely breathing, for a horrible obsession has it that the serpent has in some way made entrance into the bungalow, and I start and whirl this way and that, frightfully fearful of making a noise, though I know not why, but ever with the feeling that the thing is at my back. Then the sounds commence again and I freeze motionless.

"Now here is the only time that my consciousness, which guides my waking hours, ever in any way pierces the veil of dreams. I am, in the dream, in no way conscious that it is a dream, but, in a detached sort of way, my other mind recognizes certain facts and passes them on to my sleeping — shall I say 'ego'? That is to say, my personality is for an instant truly dual and separate to an extent, as the right and left arms are separate, while making up parts in the same entity. My dreaming mind has no cognizance of my higher mind; for the time being the other mind is subordinated and the subconscious mind is in full control, to such an extent that it does not even recognize the existence of the other. But the conscious mind, now sleeping, is cognizant of dim thought-waves emanating from the dream mind. I know that I have not made this entirely clear, but the fact remains that I know that my mind, conscious and subconscious, is near to ruin. My obsession of fear, as I stand there in my dream, is that the serpent will raise itself and peer into the window at me. And I know, in my dream, that if this occurs I shall go insane. And so vivid is the impression imparted to my conscious, now sleeping mind that the thought-waves stir the dim seas of sleep, and somehow I can feel my sanity rocking as my sanity rocks in my dream. Back and forth it totters and sways until the motion takes on a physical aspect and I in my dream am swaying from side to side. Not always is the sensation the same, but I tell you, if that horror ever raises it terrible shape and leers at me, if I ever see the fearful thing in my dream, I shall become stark, wild insane." There was a restless movement among the rest.

"God! but what a prospect!" he muttered. "To be insane and forever dreaming that same dream, night and day! But there I stand, and centuries go by, but at last a dim gray light begins to steal through the windows, the swishing dies away in the distance and presently a red, haggard sun climbs the eastern sky. Then I turn about and gaze into a mirror — and my hair has become perfectly white. I stagger to the door and fling it wide. There is nothing in sight but a wide track leading away down the hill through the grass-lands — in the opposite direction from that which I would take toward the coast. And with a shriek of maniacal laughter, I dash down the hill and race across the grasslands. I race until I drop from exhaustion, then I lie until I can stagger up and go on.

"All day I keep this up, with superhuman effort, spurred on by the horror behind me. And ever as I hurl myself forward on weakening legs, ever as I lie gasping for breath, I watch the sun with a terrible eagerness. How swiftly the sun travels when a man races it for life! A losing race it is, as I know when I watch the sun sinking toward the skyline, and the hills which I had to gain ere sundown seemingly as far away as ever."

His voice was lowered and instinctively we leaned toward him; he was gripping the chair arms and the blood was seeping from his lip.

"Then the sun sets and the shadows come and I stagger on and fall and rise and reel on again. And I laugh, laugh, laugh! Then I cease, for the moon comes up and throws the grasslands in ghostly and silvery relief. The light is white across the land, though the moon itself is like blood. And I look back the way I have come — and far — back" — all of us leaned farther toward him, our hair a-prickle; his voice came like a ghostly whisper — "far back — I — see — the — grass — waving. There is no breeze, but the tall grass parts and sways in the moonlight, in a narrow, sinuous line — far away, but nearing every instant." His voice died away.

Somebody broke the ensuing stillness: "And then —?"

"Then I awake. Never yet have I seen the foul monster. But that is the dream that haunts me, and from which I have wakened, in my childhood screaming, in my manhood in cold sweat. At irregular intervals I dream it, and each time, lately" — he hesitated and then went on — "each time lately, the thing has been getting closer — closer — the waving of the grass marks his progress and he nears me with each dream; and when he reaches me, then —"

He stopped short, then without a word rose abruptly and entered the house. The rest of us sat silent for awhile, then followed him, for it was late.

How long I slept I do not know, but I woke suddenly with the impression that somewhere in the house someone had laughed long, loud and hideously, as a maniac laughs. Starting up, wondering if I had been dreaming, I rushed from my room, just as a truly horrible shriek echoed through the house. The place was now alive with other people who had been awakened, and all of us rushed to Famings's room, whence the sounds had seemed to come.

Faming lay dead upon the floor, where it seemed he had fallen in some terrific struggle. There was no mark upon him, but his face was terribly distorted; as the face of a man who had been crushed by some superhuman force — such as some gigantic snake.

THE HYENA

Weird Tales, March 1928

From the time when I first saw Senecoza, the fetish-man, I distrusted him, and from vague distrust the idea eventually grew into hatred.

I was but newly come to the East Coast, new to African ways, somewhat inclined to follow my impulses, and possessed of a large amount of curiosity.

Because I came from Virginia, race instinct and prejudice were strong in me, and doubtless the feeling of inferiority which Senecoza constantly inspired in me had a great deal to do with my antipathy for him.

He was surprisingly tall, and leanly built. Six inches above six feet he stood, and so muscular was his spare frame that he weighed a good two hundred pounds. His weight seemed incredible when one looked at his lanky build, but he was all muscle — a lean, black giant. His features were not pure Negro. They more resembled Berber than Bantu, with the high, bulging forehead, thin nose and thin, straight lips. But his hair was as kinky as a Bushman's and his color was blacker even than the Masai. In fact, his glossy hide had a different hue from those of the native tribesmen, and I believe that he was of a different tribe.

It was seldom that we of the ranch saw him. Then without warning he would be among us, or we would see him striding through the shoulder-high grass of the veldt, sometimes alone, sometimes followed at a respectful distance by several of the wilder Masai, who bunched up at a distance from the buildings, grasping their spears nervously and eyeing everyone suspiciously. He would make his greetings with a courtly grace; his manner was deferentially courteous, but somehow it "rubbed me the wrong way," so to speak. I always had a vague feeling that the black was mocking us. He would stand before us, a naked bronze giant; make trade for a few simple articles, such as a copper kettle, beads or a trade musket; repeat words of some chief, and take his departure.

I did not like him. And being young and impetuous, I spoke my opinion to Ludtvik Strolvaus, a very distant relative, tenth cousin or suchlike, on whose trading-post ranch I was staying.

But Ludtvik chuckled in his blond beard and said that the

fetish-man was all right.

"A power he is among the natives, true. They all fear him. But a friend he is to the whites. *Ja.*"

Ludtvik was long a resident on the East Coast; he knew natives and he knew the fat Australian cattle he raised, but he had little imagination.

The ranch buildings were in the midst of a stockade, on a kind of slope, overlooking countless miles on miles of the finest grazing land in Africa. The stockade was large, well suited for defense. Most of the thousand cattle could be driven inside in case of an uprising of the Masai. Ludtvik was inordinately proud of his cattle.

"One thousand now," he would tell me, his round face beaming, "one thousand now. But later, ah! Ten thousand and another ten thousand. This is a good beginning, but only a beginning. *Ja.*"

I must confess that I got little thrill out of the cattle. Natives herded and corralled them; all Ludtvik and I had to do was to ride about and give orders. That was the work he liked best, and I left it mostly to him.

My chief sport was in riding away across the veldt, alone or attended by a gun-bearer, with a rifle. Not that I ever bagged much game. In the first place I was an execrable marksman; I could hardly have hit an elephant at close range. In the second place, it seemed to me a shame to shoot so many things. A bush-antelope would bound up in front of me and race away, and I would sit watching him, admiring the slim, lithe figure, thrilled with the graceful beauty of the creature, my rifle lying idle across my saddle horn.

The native boy who served as my gun-bearer began to suspect that I was deliberately refraining from shooting, and he began in a covert way to throw sneering hints about my womanishness. I was young and valued even the opinion of a native; which is very foolish. His remarks stung my pride, and one day I hauled him off his horse and pounded him until he yelled for mercy. Thereafter my doings were not questioned.

But still I felt inferior when in the presence of the fetish-man. I could not get the other natives to talk about him. All I could get out of them was a scared rolling of the eyeballs, gesticulation indicative of fear, and vague information that the fetish-man dwelt among the tribes some distance in the interior. General opinion seemed to be that Senecoza was a good man to let alone.

One incident made the mystery about the fetish-man take on, it seemed, a rather sinister form.

In the mysterious way that news travels in Africa, and which white men so seldom hear of, we learned that Senecoza and a minor chief had had a falling out of some kind. It was vague and seemed to have no especial basis of fact. But shortly afterward that chief was found half-devoured by hyenas. That, in itself, was not unusual, but the fright with which the natives heard the news was. The chief was nothing to them; in fact he was something of a villain, but his killing seemed to inspire them with a fright that was little short of homicidal. When the black reaches a certain stage of fear, he is as dangerous as a cornered panther. The next time Senecoza called, they rose and fled en masse and did not return until he had taken his departure.

Between the fear of the blacks, the tearing to pieces of the chief by the hyenas, and the fetish-man, I seemed to sense vaguely a connection of some kind. But I could not grasp the intangible thought.

Not long thereafter, that thought was intensified by another incident. I had ridden far out on the veldt, accompanied by my servant. As we paused to rest our horses close to a kopje, I saw, upon the top, a hyena eyeing us. Rather surprised, for the beasts are not in the habit of thus boldly approaching man in the daytime, I raised my rifle and was taking a steady aim, for I always hated the things, when my servant caught my arm.

"No shoot, *bwana*! No shoot!" he exclaimed hastily, jabbering a great deal in his own language, with which I was not familiar.

"What's up?" I asked impatiently.

He kept on jabbering and pulling my arm, until I gathered that the hyena was a fetish-beast of some kind.

"Oh, all right," I conceded, lowering my rifle just as the hyena turned and sauntered out of sight.

Something about the lank, repulsive beast and his shambling yet gracefully lithe walk struck my sense of humor with a ludicrous comparison.

Laughing, I pointed toward the beast and said, "That fellow looks like a hyena-imitation of Senecoza, the fetish-man." My simple statement seemed to throw the native into a more abject fear than ever.

He turned his pony and dashed off in the general direction of the ranch, looking back at me with a scared face.

I followed, annoyed. And as I rode I pondered. Hyenas, a fetish-man, a chief torn to pieces, a countryside of natives in fear; what was the connection? I puzzled and puzzled, but I was new to Africa; I was young and impatient, and presently with a shrug of annoyance I discarded the whole problem.

The next time Senecoza came to the ranch, he managed to stop directly in front of me. For a fleeting instant his glittering eyes looked into mine. And in spite of myself, I shuddered and stepped back, involuntarily, feeling much as a man feels who looks un-aware into the eyes of a serpent. There was nothing tangible, nothing on which I could base a quarrel, but there was a distinct threat. Before my Nordic pugnacity could reassert itself, he was gone. I said nothing. But I knew that Senecoza hated me for some reason and that he plotted my killing. Why, I did not know.

As for me, my distrust grew into bewildered rage, which in turn became hate.

And then Ellen Farel came to the ranch. Why she should choose a trading-ranch in East Africa for a place to rest from the society life of New York, I do not know. Africa is no place for a woman. That is what Ludtvik, also a cousin of hers, told her, but he was overjoyed to see her. As for me, girls never interested me much; usually I felt like a fool in their presence and was glad to be out. But there were few whites in the vicinity and I tired of the company of Ludtvik.

Ellen was standing on the wide veranda when I first saw her, a slim, pretty young thing, with rosy cheeks and hair like gold and large gray eyes. She was surprisingly winsome in her costume of riding-breeches, puttees, jacket and light helmet.

I felt extremely awkward, dusty and stupid as I sat on my wiry African pony and stared at her.

She saw a stocky youth of medium height, with sandy hair, eyes in which a kind of gray predominated; an ordinary, unhandsome youth, clad in dusty riding-clothes and a cartridge belt on one side of which was slung an ancient Colt of big caliber, and on the other a long, wicked hunting-knife.

I dismounted, and she came forward, hand outstretched.

"I'm Ellen," she said, "and I know you're Steve. Cousin Ludtvik has been telling me about you."

I shook hands, surprised at the thrill the mere touch of her hand gave me.

She was enthusiastic about the ranch. She was enthusiastic about everything. Seldom have I seen anyone who had more vigor and vim, more enjoyment of everything done. She fairly scintillated with mirth and gaiety.

Ludtvik gave her the best horse on the place, and we rode much about the ranch and over the veldt.

The blacks interested her much. They were afraid of her, not being used to white women. She would have been off her horse and playing with the pickaninnies if I had let her. She couldn't understand why she should treat the black people as dust beneath her feet. We had long arguments about it. I could not convince her, so I told her bluntly that she didn't know anything about it and she must do as I told her.

She pouted her pretty lips and called me a tyrant, and then was off over the veldt like an antelope, laughing at me over her shoulder, her hair blowing free in the breeze.

Tyrant! I was her slave from the first. Somehow the idea of becoming a lover never enter my mind. It was not the fact that she was several years older than I, or that she had a sweetheart (several of them, I think) back in New York. Simply, I worshipped her; her presence intoxicated me, and I could think of no more enjoyable existence than serving her as a devoted slave.

I was mending a saddle one day when she came running in.

"Oh, Steve!" she called; "there's the most romantic-looking savage! Come quick and tell me what his name is."

She led me out of the veranda.

"There he is," she said, naively pointing. Arms folded, haughty head thrown back, stood Senecoza.

Ludtvik who was talking to him, paid no attention to the girl until he had completed his business with the fetish-man; and then, turning, he took her arm and they went into the house together.

Again I was face to face with the savage; but this time he was not looking at me. With a rage amounting almost to madness, I saw that he was gazing after the girl. There was an expression in his serpentlike eyes —

On the instant my gun was out and leveled. My hand shook like a leaf with the intensity of my fury. Surely I must shoot Senecoza down like the snake he was, shoot him down and riddle him, shoot him into a shredded heap!

The fleeting expression left his eyes and they were fixed on me. Detached they seemed, inhuman in their sardonic calm. And I could not pull the trigger.

For a moment we stood, and then he turned and strode away, a magnificent figure, while I glared after him and snarled with helpless fury.

I sat down on the veranda. What a man of mystery was that savage! What strange power did he possess? Was I right, I wondered, in interpreting the fleeting expression as he gazed after the girl? It seemed to me, in my youth and folly, incredible that a black man, no matter what his rank, should look at a white woman as he did. Most astonishing of all, why could I not shoot him down?

I started as a hand touched my arm.

"What are thinking about, Steve?" asked Ellen, laughing. Then before I could say anything, "Wasn't that chief, or whatever he was, a fine specimen of a savage? He invited us to come to his kraal; is that what you call it? It's away off in the veldt somewhere, and we're going."

"No!" I exclaimed violently, springing up.

"Why Steve," she gasped recoiling, "how rude! He's a perfect gentleman, isn't he, Cousin Ludtvik?"

"*Ja*," nodded Ludtvik, placidly, "we go to his kraal sometime soon, maybe. A strong chief, that savage. His chief has perhaps good trade."

"No!" I repeated furiously. "*I'll* go if somebody has to! Ellen's not going near that beast!"

"Well, that's nice!" remarked Ellen, somewhat indignantly. "I guess you're my boss, mister man?"

With all her sweetness, she had a mind of her own. In spite of all I could do, they arranged to go to the fetish-man's village the next day.

That night the girl came out to me, where I sat on the veranda in the moonlight, and she sat down on the arm of my chair.

"You're not angry at me, are you, Steve?" she said, wistfully, putting her arm around my shoulders. "Not mad, are you?"

Mad? Yes, maddened by the touch of her soft body — such mad devotion as a slave feels. I wanted to grovel in the dust at her feet and kiss her dainty shoes. Will women never learn the effect they have on men?

I took her hand hesitantly and pressed it to my lips. I think she must have sensed some of my devotion.

"Dear Steve," she murmured, and the words were like a caress, "come, let's walk in the moonlight."

We walked outside the stockade. I should have known better, for I had no weapon but the big Turkish dagger I carried and used for a hunting-knife, but she wished to.

"Tell me about this Senecoza," she asked, and I welcomed the opportunity. And then I thought: what could I tell her? That hyenas had eaten a small chief of the Masai? That the natives feared the fetish-man? That he had looked at her?

And then the girl screamed as out of the tall grass leaped a vague shape, half-seen in the moonlight.

I felt a heavy, hairy form crash against my shoulders; keen fangs ripped my upflung arm. I went to the earth, fighting with frenzied horror. My jacket was slit to ribbons and the fangs were at my throat before I found and drew my knife and stabbed, blindly and savagely. I felt my blade rip into my foe, and then, like a shadow, it was gone. I staggered to my feet, somewhat shaken. The girl caught and steadied me.

"What was it?" she gasped, leading me toward the stockade.

"A hyena," I answered. "I could tell by the scent. But I never heard of one attacking like that."

She shuddered. Later on, after my torn arm had been bandaged, she came close to me and said in a wondrously subdued voice, "Steve, I've decided not to go to the village, if you don't want me to."

After the wounds on my arm had become scars Ellen and I resumed our rides, as might be expected. One day we had wandered rather far out on the veldt, and she challenged me to a race. Her horse easily distanced mine, and she stopped and waited for me, laughing.

She had stopped on a sort of kopje, and she pointed to a clump of trees some distance away.

"Trees!" she said gleefully. "Let's ride down there. There are so few trees on the veldt."

And she dashed away. I followed some instinctive caution, loosening my pistol in its holster, and, drawing my knife, I thrust down in my boot so that it was entirely concealed.

We were perhaps halfway to the trees when from the tall grass about us leaped Senecoza and some twenty warriors.

One seized the girl's bridle and the others rushed me. The one who caught at Ellen went down with a bullet between his eyes, and another crumpled at my second shot. Then a thrown war-club hurled me from the saddle, half-senseless, and as the blacks closed in on me I saw Ellen's horse, driven frantic by the prick of a carelessly handled spear, scream and rear, scattering the blacks who held her, and dash away at headlong speed, the bit in her teeth.

I saw Senecoza leap on my horse and give chase, flinging a savage command over his shoulder; and both vanished over the kopje.

The warriors bound me hand and foot and carried me into the trees. A hut stood among them — a native hut of thatch and bark. Somehow the sight of it set me shuddering. It seemed to lurk, repellent and indescribably malevolent amongst the trees; to hint of horrid and obscene rites; of voodoo.

I know not why it is, but the sight of a native hut, alone and hidden, far from a village or tribe, always has to me a suggestion of nameless horror. Perhaps that is because only a black who is crazed or one who is so criminal that he has been exiled by his tribe will dwell that way.

In front of the hut they threw me down.

"When Senecoza returns with the girl," said they, "you will enter." And they laughed like fiends. Then, leaving one black to see that I did not escape, they left.

The black who remained kicked me viciously; he was a bestial-looking Negro, armed with a trade-musket.

"They go to kill white men, fool!" he mocked me. "They go to the ranches and trading-posts, first to that fool of an Englishman." Meaning Smith, the owner of a neighboring ranch.

And he went on giving details. Senecoza had made the plot, he boasted. They would chase all the white men to the coast.

"Senecoza is more than a man," he boasted. "You shall see, white man," lowering his voice and glancing about him, from beneath his low, beetling brows; "you shall see the magic of Senecoza." And he grinned, disclosing teeth filed to points.

"Cannibal!" I ejaculated, involuntarily. "A Masai?"

"No," he answered. "A man of Senecoza."

"Who will kill no white men," I jeered.

He scowled savagely. "I will kill you, white man."

"You dare not."

"That is true," he admitted, and added angrily, "Senecoza will kill you himself."

And meantime Ellen was riding like mad, gaining on the fetish-man, but unable to ride toward the ranch, for he had gotten between and was forcing her steadily out upon the veldt.

The black unfastened my bonds. His line of reasoning was easy to see; absurdly easy. He could not kill a prisoner of the fetish-man, but he could kill him to prevent his escape. And he was maddened with the blood-lust. Stepping back, he half-raised his trade-musket, watching me as a snake watches a rabbit.

It must have been about that time, as she afterward told me, that Ellen's horse stumbled and threw her. Before she could rise, the black had leaped from his horse and seized her in his arms. She screamed and fought, but he gripped her, held her helpless and laughed at her. Tearing her jacket to pieces, he bound her arms and legs, remounted and started back, carrying the half-fainting girl in front of him.

Back in front of the hut I rose slowly. I rubbed my arms where the ropes had been, moved a little closer to the black, stretched, stooped and rubbed my legs; then with a catlike bound I was on him, my knife flashing from my boot. The trade-musket crashed and the charge whizzed above my head as I knocked up the barrel and closed with him. Hand to hand, I would have been no match for the black giant; but I had the knife. Clinched close together we were too close for him to use the trade-musket for a club. He wasted time trying to do that, and with a desperate effort I threw him off his balance and drove the dagger to the hilt in his black chest.

I wrenched it out again; I had no other weapon, for I could find no more ammunition for the trade-musket.

I had no idea which way Ellen had fled. I assumed she had gone toward the ranch, and in that direction I took my way. Smith must be warned. The warriors were far ahead of me. Even then they might be creeping up about the unsuspecting ranch.

I had not covered a fourth of the distance, when a drumming of hoofs behind me caused me to turn my head. Ellen's horse was thundering toward me, riderless. I caught her as she raced past me, and managed to stop her. The story was plain. The girl had either reached a place of safety and had turned the horse loose, or what was much more likely, had been captured, the horse escaping and fleeing toward the ranch, as a horse will do. I gripped the saddle, torn with indecision. Finally I leaped on the horse and sent her flying toward Smith's ranch. It was not many miles; Smith must not be massacred by those black devils, and I must find a gun if I escaped to rescue the girl from Senecoza.

A half-mile from Smith's I overtook the raiders and went through them like drifting smoke. The workers at Smith's place were startled by a wild-riding horseman charging headlong into the stockade, shouting, "Masai! Masai! A raid, you fools!" snatching a gun and flying out again.

So when the savages arrived they found everybody ready for them, and they got such a warm reception that after one attempt they turned tail and fled back across the veldt.

And I was riding as I never rode before. The mare was almost exhausted, but I pushed her mercilessly. On, on!

I aimed for the only place I knew likely. The hut among the trees. I assumed that the fetish-man would return there.

And long before the hut came into sight, a horseman dashed from the grass, going at right angles to my course, and our horses, colliding, sent both tired animals to the ground.

"Steve!" It was a cry of joy mingled with fear. Ellen lay, tied hand and foot, gazing up at me wildly as I regained my feet.

Senecoza came with a rush, his long knife flashing in the sunlight. Back and forth we fought — slash, ward and parry, my ferocity and agility matching his savagery and skill.

A terrific lunge which he aimed at me, I caught on my point, laying his arm open, and then with a quick engage and wrench, disarmed him. But before I could use my advantage, he sprang away into the grass and vanished.

I caught up the girl, slashing her bonds, and she clung to me, poor child, until I lifted her and carried her toward the horses. But we were not yet through with Senecoza. He must have had a rifle cached away somewhere in the bush, for the first I knew of him was when a bullet spat within a foot above my head.

I caught at the bridles, and then I saw that the mare had done all she could, temporarily. She was exhausted. I swung Ellen up on the horse.

"Ride for our ranch," I ordered her. "The raiders are out, but you can get through. Ride low and ride fast!"

"But you, Steve!"

"Go, go!" I ordered, swinging her horse around and starting it. She dashed away, looking at me wistfully over her shoulder. Then I snatched the rifle and a handful of cartridges I had gotten at Smith's, and took to the bush. And through the hot African day, Senecoza and I played a game of hide-and-seek. Crawling, slipping in and out of the scanty veldt-bushes, crouching in the tall grass, we traded shots back and forth. A movement of the grass, a snapping twig, the rasp of grass-blades, and a bullet came questing, another answering it.

I had but a few cartridges and I fired carefully, but presently I pushed my one remaining cartridge into the rifle — a big, six-bore, single-barrel breech-loader, for I had not had time to pick when I snatched it up.

I crouched in my covert and watched for the black to betray himself by a careless movement. Not a sound, not a whisper among the grasses. Away off over the veldt a hyena sounded his fiendish laugh and another answered, closer at hand. The cold sweat broke out on my brow.

What was that? A drumming of many horses' hoofs! Raiders returning? I ventured a look and could have shouted for joy. At least twenty men were sweeping toward me, white men and ranch-boys, and ahead of them all rode Ellen! They were still some distance away. I darted behind a tall bush and rose, waving my hand to attract their attention.

They shouted and pointed to something beyond me. I whirled and saw, some thirty yards away, a huge hyena slinking toward me, rapidly. I glanced carefully across the veldt. Somewhere out there, hidden by the billowing grasses, lurked Senecoza. A shot would betray to him my position — and I had but one cartridge. The rescue party was still out of range.

I looked again at the hyena. He was still rushing toward me. There was no doubt as to his intentions. His eyes glittered like a fiend's from Hell, and a scar on his shoulder showed him to be the same beast that had once before attacked me. Then a kind of horror took hold of me, and resting the old elephant rifle over my elbow, I sent my last bullet crashing through the bestial thing. With a scream that seemed to have a horribly human note in it, the hyena turned and fled back into the bush, reeling as it ran.

And the rescue party swept up around me.

A fusillade of bullets crashed through the bush from which

Senecoza had sent his last shot. There was no reply.

"Ve hunt ter snake down," quoth Cousin Ludtvik, his Boer accent increasing with his excitement. And we scattered through the veldt in a skirmish line, combing every inch of it warily.

Not a trace of the fetish-man did we find. A rifle we found, empty, with empty shells scattered about, and (which was very strange) *hyena tracks leading away from the rifle.*

I felt the short hairs of my neck bristle with intangible horror. We looked at each other, and said not a word, as with a tacit agreement we took up the trail of the hyena.

We followed it as it wound in and out in the shoulder-high grass, showing how it had slipped up on me, stalking me as a tiger stalks its victim. We struck the trail the thing had made, returning to the bush after I had shot it. Splashes of blood marked the way it had taken. We followed.

"It leads toward the fetish-hut," muttered an Englishman. "Here, sirs, is a damnable mystery."

And Cousin Ludtvik ordered Ellen to stay back, leaving two men with her.

We followed the trail over the kopje and into the clump of trees. Straight to the door of the hut it led. We circled the hut cautiously, but no tracks led away. It was inside the hut. Rifles ready, we forced the rude door.

No tracks led away from the hut and no tracks led to it except the tracks of the hyena. Yet there was no hyena within that hut; and on the dirt floor, a bullet through his black breast, lay Senecoza, the fetish-man.

REMEMBRANCE

Weird Tales, April 1928

Eight thousand years ago a man I slew;
  I lay in wait beside a sparkling rill
  There in an upland valley green and still.
The white stream gurgled where the rushes grew;
The hills were veiled in dreamy hazes blue.
    He came along the trail; with savage skill
    My spear leaped like a snake to make my kill –
Leaped like a striking snake and pierced him through.

And still when blue haze dreams along the sky
    And breezes bring the murmur of the sea,
A whisper thrills me where at ease I lie
    Beneath the branches of some mountain tree;
He comes, fog-dim, the ghost that will not die,
    And with accusing finger points at me.

SEA CURSE

Weird Tales, May 1928

And some return by the failing light
And some in the waking dream,
For she hears the heels of the dripping ghosts
That ride the rough roofbeam.

                     — Kipling.

They were the brawlers and braggarts, the loud boasters and hard drinkers, of Faring town, John Kulrek and his crony Lie-lip Canool. Many a time have I, a tousled-haired lad, stolen to the tavern door to listen to their curses, their profane arguments and wild sea songs; half-fearful and half in admiration of these wild rovers. Aye, all the people of Faring town gazed on them with fear and admiration, for they were not like the rest of the Faring men; they were not content to ply their trade along the coasts and among the shark-teeth shoals. No yawls, no skiffs for them! They fared far, farther than any other man in the village, for they shipped on the great sailing-ships that went out on the white tides to brave the restless gray ocean and make ports in strange lands.

Ah, I mind it was swift times in the little seacoast village of Faring when John Kulrek came home, with his furtive Lie-lip at his side, swaggering down the gangplank, in his tarry sea-clothes, and the broad leather belt that held his ever-ready dagger; shouting condescending greeting to some favored acquaintance, kissing some maiden who ventured too near; then up the street, roaring some scarcely decent song of the sea. How the cringers and the idlers, the hangers-on, would swarm about the two desperate heroes, flattering and smirking, guffawing hilariously at each nasty jest. For to the tavern loafers and to some of the weaker among the straightforward villagers, these men with their wild talk and their brutal deeds, their tales of the Seven Seas and the far countries, these men, I say, were valiant knights, nature's noblemen who dared to be men of blood and brawn.

And all feared them, so that when a man was beaten or a woman insulted, the villagers muttered — and did nothing. And so when Moll Farrell's niece was put to shame by John Kulrek, none dared even to put in words what all thought. Moll had never married, and she and the girl lived alone in a little hut down close to the beach, so close that in high tide the waves came almost to the door.

The people of the village accounted old Moll something of a witch, and she was a grim, gaunt old dame who had little to say to anyone. But she minded her own business, and eked out a slim living by gathering clams, and picking up bits of driftwood.

The girl was a pretty, foolish little thing, vain and easily befooled, else she had never yielded to the shark-like blandishments of John Kulrek.

I mind the day was a cold winter day with a sharp breeze out of the east when the old dame came into the village street shrieking that the girl had vanished. All scattered over the beach and back among the bleak inland hills to search for her — all save John Kulrek and his cronies who sat in the tavern dicing and toping. All the while beyond the shoals, we heard the never-ceasing droning of the heaving, restless grey monster, and in the dim light of the ghostly dawn Moll Farrell's girl came home.

The tides bore her gently across the wet sands and laid her almost at her own door. Virgin-white she was, and her arms were folded across her still bosom; calm was her face, and the gray tides sighed about her slender limbs. Moll Farrell's eyes were stones, yet she stood above her dead girl and spoke no word till John Kulrek and his crony came reeling down from the tavern, their drinking-jacks still in their hands. Drunk was John Kulrek, and the people gave back for him, murder in their souls; so he came and laughed at Moll Farrell across the body of her girl.

"Zounds!" swore John Kulrek; "The wench has drowned herself, Lie-lip!"

Lie-lip laughed, with the twist of his thin mouth. He always hated Moll Farrell, for it was she that had given him the name of Lie-lip.

Then John Kulrek lifted his drinking-jack, swaying on his uncertain legs. "A health to the wench's ghost!" he bellowed, while all stood aghast.

Then Moll Farrell spoke, and the words broke from her in a scream which sent ripples of cold up and down the spines of the throng.

"The curse of the Foul Fiend upon you, John Kulrek!" she screamed. "The curse of God rest upon your vile soul throughout eternity! May you gaze on sights that shall sear the eyes of you and scorch the soul of you! May you die a bloody death and writhe in Hell's flames for a million and a million and yet a million years! I curse you by sea and by land, by earth and by air, by the demons of the oceans and the demons of the swamplands, the fiends of the forests and the goblins of the hills! And you" — her lean finger stabbed at Lie-lip Canool and he started backward, his face paling — "you shall be the death of John Kulrek and he shall be the death of you! You shall bring John Kulrek to the doors of Hell and John Kulrek shall bring you to the gallows-tree! I set the seal of death upon your brow, John Kulrek! You shall live in terror and die in horror far out upon the cold grey sea! But the sea that took the soul of innocence to her bosom shall not take you, but shall fling forth your vile carcass to the sands! Aye, John Kulrek" — and she spoke with such a terrible intensity that the drunken mockery on the man's face changed to one of swinish stupidity — "the sea roars for the victim it will not keep! There is snow upon the hills, John Kulrek, and ere it melts your corpse will lie at my feet. And I shall spit upon it and be content."

Kulrek and his crony sailed at dawn for a long voyage, and Moll went back to her hut and her clam gathering. She seemed to grow leaner and more grim than ever and her eyes smoldered with a light not sane. The days glided by and people whispered among themselves that Moll's days were numbered, for she faded to a ghost of a woman; but she went her way, refusing all aid.

That was a short, cold summer and the snow on the barren inland hills never melted; a thing very unusual, which caused much comment among the villagers. At dusk and at dawn Moll would come up on the beach, gaze up at the snow which glittered on the hills, then out to sea with a fierce intensity in her gaze.

Then the days grew shorter, the nights longer and darker, and the cold grey tides came sweeping along the bleak strands, bearing the rain and sleet of the sharp east breezes.

And upon a bleak day a trading-vessel sailed into the bay and anchored. And all the idlers and the wastrels flocked to the wharfs, for that was the ship upon which John Kulrek and Lie-lip Canool had sailed. Down the gangplank came Lie-lip, more furtive than ever, but John Kulrek was not there.

To shouted queries, Canool shook his head. "Kulrek deserted ship at a port of Sumatra," said he. "He had a row with the skipper, lads; wanted me to desert, too, but no! I had to see you fine lads again, eh, boys?"

Almost cringing was Lie-lip Canool, and suddenly he recoiled as Moll Farrell came through the throng. A moment they stood eyeing each other; then Moll's grim lips bent in a terrible smile.

"There's blood on your hand, Canool!" she lashed out suddenly — so suddenly that Lie-lip started and rubbed his right hand across his left sleeve.

"Stand aside, witch!" he snarled in sudden anger, striding through the crowd which gave back for him. His admirers followed him to the tavern.

Now, I mind that the next day was even colder; grey fogs came drifting out of the east and veiled the sea and the beaches. There would be no sailing that day, and so all the villagers were in their snug houses or matching tales at the tavern. So it came about that Joe, my friend, a lad of my own age, and I, were the ones who saw the first of the strange thing that happened.

Being harum-scarum lads of no wisdom, we were sitting in a small rowboat, floating at the end of the wharfs, each shivering and wishing the other would suggest leaving, there being no reason whatever for our being there, save that it was a good place to build air-castles undisturbed.

Suddenly Joe raised his hand. "Say," he said, "d'ye hear? Who can be out on the bay upon a day like this?"

"Nobody. What d'ye hear?"

"Oars. Or I'm a lubber. Listen."

There was no seeing anything in that fog, and I heard nothing. Yet Joe swore he did, and suddenly his face assumed a strange look.

"Somebody rowing out there, I tell you! The bay is alive with oars from the sound! A score of boats at the least! Ye dolt, can ye not hear?"

Then, as I shook my head, he leaped and began to undo the painter.

"I'm off to see. Name me liar if the bay is not full of boats, all together like a close fleet. Are you with me?"

Yes, I was with him, though I heard nothing. Then out in the greyness we went, and the fog closed behind and before so that we drifted in a vague world of smoke, seeing naught and hearing naught. We were lost in no time, and I cursed Joe for leading us upon a wild goose chase that was like to end with our being swept out to sea. I thought of Moll Farrell's girl and shuddered.

How long we drifted I know not. Minutes faded into hours, hours into centuries. Still Joe swore he heard the oars, now close at hand, now far away, and for hours we followed them, steering our course toward the sound, as the noise grew or receded. This I later thought of, and could not understand.

Then, when my hands were so numb that I could no longer hold the oar, and the forerunning drowsiness of cold and exhaustion was stealing over me, bleak white stars broke through the fog which glided suddenly away, fading like a ghost of smoke, and we found ourselves afloat just outside the mouth of the bay. The waters lay smooth as a pond, all dark green and silver in the starlight, and the cold came crisper than ever. I was swinging the boat about, to put back into the bay, when Joe gave a shout, and for the first time I heard the clack of oarlocks. I glanced over my shoulder and my blood went cold.

A great beaked prow loomed above us, a weird, unfamiliar shape against the stars, and as I caught my breath, sheered sharply and swept by us, with a curious swishing I never heard any other craft make. Joe screamed and backed oars frantically, and the boat walled out of the way just in time; for though the prow had missed us, still otherwise we had died. For from the sides of the ship stood long oars, bank upon bank which swept her along. Though I had never seen such a craft, I knew her for a galley. But what was she doing upon our coasts? They said, the far-farers, that such ships were still in use among the heathens of Barbary; but it was many along, heaving mile to Barbary, and even so she did not resemble the ships described by those who had sailed far.

We started in pursuit, and this was strange, for though the waters broke about her prow, and she seemed fairly to fly through the waves, yet she was making little speed, and it was no time before we caught up with her. Making our painter fast to a chain far back beyond the reach of the swishing oars, we hailed those on deck. But there came no answer, and at last, conquering our fears, we clambered up the chain and found ourselves upon the strangest deck man has trod for many a long, roaring century.

"This is no Barbary rover!" muttered Joe fearsomely. "Look, how old it seems! Almost ready to fall to pieces. Why, 'tis fairly rotten!"

There was no one on deck, no one at the long sweep with which the craft was steered. We stole to the hold and looked down the stair. Then and there, if ever men were on the verge of insanity, it was we. For there were rowers there, it is true; they sat upon the rowers' benches and drove the creaking oars through the gray waters. *And they that rowed were skeletons!*

Shrieking, we plunged across the deck, to fling ourselves into the sea. But at the rail I tripped upon something and fell headlong, and as I lay, I saw a thing which vanquished my fear of the horrors below for an instant. The thing upon which I had tripped was a human body, and in the dim gray light that was beginning to steal across the eastern waves I saw a dagger hilt standing up between his shoulders. Joe was at the rail, urging me to haste, and together we slid down the chain and cut the painter.

Then we stood off into the bay. Straight on kept the grim galley, and we followed, slowly, wondering. She seemed to be heading straight for the beach beside the wharfs, and as we approached, we saw the wharfs thronged with people. They had missed us, no doubt, and now they stood, there in the early dawn light, struck dumb by the apparition which had come up out of the night and the grim ocean.

Straight on swept the galley, her oars a-swish; then ere she reached the shallow water — crash! — a terrific reverberation shook the bay. Before our eyes the grim craft seemed to melt away; then she vanished, and the green waters seethed where she had ridden, but there floated no driftwood there, nor did there ever float any ashore. Aye, something floated ashore, but it was grim driftwood!

We made the landing amid a hum of excited conversation that stopped suddenly. Moll Farrell stood before her hut, limned gauntly against the ghostly dawn, her lean hand pointing seaward. And across the sighing wet sands, borne by the grey tide, something came floating; something that the waves dropped at Moll Farrell's feet. And there looked up at us, as we crowded about, a pair of unseeing eyes set in a still, white face. John Kulrek had come home.

Still and grim he lay, rocked by the tide, and as he lurched sideways, all saw the dagger hilt that stood from his back — the dagger all of us had seen a thousand times at the belt of Lie-lip Canool.

"Aye, I killed him!" came Canool's shriek, as he writhed and groveled before our gaze. "At sea on a still night in a drunken brawl I slew him and hurled him overboard! And from the far seas he has followed me" — his voice sank to a hideous whisper — "because — of — the — curse — the — sea — would — not — keep — his — body!"

And the wretch sank down, trembling, the shadow of the gallows already in his eyes.

"Aye!" Strong, deep and exultant was Moll Farrell's voice. "From the hell of lost craft Satan sent a ship of bygone ages! A ship red with gore and stained with the memory of horrid crimes! None other would bear such a vile carcass! The sea has taken vengeance and has given me mine. See now, how I spit upon the face of John Kulrek."

And with a ghastly laugh, she pitched forward, the blood starting to her lips. And the sun came up across the restless sea.

THE GATES OF NINEVEH

Weird Tales, July 1928

These are the gates of Nineveh; here
   Sargon came when his wars were won,
Gazed at the turrets looming clear,
   Boldly etched in the morning sun.

Down from his chariot Sargon came,
   Tossed his helmet upon the sand,
Dropped his sword with its blade like flame,
   Stroked his beard with his empty hand.

"Towers are flaunting their banners red,
   The people greet me with song and mirth,
But a weird is on me," Sargon said,
   "And I see the end of the tribes of earth.

"Cities crumble, and chariots rust —
   I see through a fog that is strange and gray —
All kingly things fade back to the dust,
   Even the gates of Nineveh."

RED SHADOWS

Weird Tales, August 1928

1. The Coming of Solomon

The moonlight shimmered hazily, making silvery mists of illusion among the shadowy trees. A faint breeze whispered down the valley, bearing a shadow that was not of the moon-mist. A faint scent of smoke was apparent.

The man whose long, swinging strides, unhurried yet unswerving, had carried him for many a mile since sunrise, stopped suddenly. A movement in the trees had caught his attention, and he moved silently toward the shadows, a hand resting lightly on the hilt of his long, slim rapier.

Warily he advanced, his eyes striving to pierce the darkness that brooded under the trees. This was a wild and menacing country; death might be lurking under those trees. Then his hand fell away from the hilt and he leaned forward. Death indeed was there, but not in such shape as might cause him fear.

"The fires of Hades!" he murmured. "A girl! What has harmed you, child? Be not afraid of me."

The girl looked up at him, her face like a dim white rose in the dark.

"You — who are — you?" her words came in gasps.

"Naught but a wanderer, a landless man, but a friend to all in need." The gentle voice sounded somehow incongruous, coming from the man.

The girl sought to prop herself up on her elbow, and instantly he knelt and raised her to a sitting position, her head resting against his shoulder. His hand touched her breast and came away red and wet.

"Tell me." His voice was soft, soothing, as one speaks to a babe.

"Le Loup," she gasped, her voice swiftly growing weaker. "He and his men — descended upon our village — a mile up the valley. They robbed — slew — burned —"

"That, then, was the smoke I scented," muttered the man. "Go on, child."

"I ran. He, the Wolf, pursued me — and — caught me —" The words died away in a shuddering silence.

"I understand, child. Then —?"

"Then — he — he — stabbed me — with his dagger — oh, blessed saints! — mercy —"

Suddenly the slim form went limp. The man eased her to the earth, and touched her brow lightly.

"Dead!" he muttered.

Slowly he rose, mechanically wiping his hands upon his cloak. A dark scowl had settled on his somber brow. Yet he made no wild, reckless vow, swore no oath by saints or devils.

"Men shall die for this," he said coldly.

2. The Lair of the Wolf

"You are a fool!" The words came in a cold snarl that curdled the hearer's blood.

He who had just been named a fool lowered his eyes sullenly without answer.

"You and all the others I lead!" The speaker leaned forward, his fist pounding emphasis on the rude table between them. He was a tall, rangy-built man, supple as a leopard and with a lean, cruel, predatory face. His eyes danced and glittered with a kind of reckless mockery.

The fellow spoken to replied sullenly, "This Solomon Kane is a demon from Hell, I tell you."

"Faugh! Dolt! He is a man — who will die from a pistol ball or a sword thrust."

"So thought Jean, Juan and La Costa," answered the other grimly. "Where are they? Ask the mountain wolves that tore the flesh from their dead bones. Where does this Kane hide? We have searched the mountains and the valleys for leagues, and we have found no trace. I tell you, Le Loup, he comes up from Hell. I knew no good would come from hanging that friar a moon ago."

The Wolf strummed impatiently upon the table. His keen face, despite lines of wild living and dissipation, was the face of a thinker. The superstitions of his followers affected him not at all.

"Faugh! I say again. The fellow has found some cavern or secret vale of which we do not know where he hides in the day."

"And at night he sallies forth and slays us," gloomily commented the other. "He hunts us down as a wolf hunts deer — by God, Le Loup, you name yourself Wolf but I think you have met at last a fiercer and more crafty wolf than yourself! The first we know of this man is when we find Jean, the most desperate bandit unhung, nailed to a tree with his own dagger through his breast, and the letters S.L.K. carved upon his dead cheeks. Then the Spaniard Juan is struck down, and after we find him he lives long enough to tell us that the slayer is an Englishman, Solomon Kane, who has sworn to destroy our entire band! What then? La Costa, a swordsman second only to yourself, goes forth swearing to meet this Kane. By the demons of perdition, it seems he met him! For we found his sword-pierced corpse upon a cliff. What now? Are we all to fall before this English fiend?"

"True, our best men have been done to death by him," mused the bandit chief. "Soon the rest return from that little trip to the hermit's; then we shall see. Kane can not hide forever. Then — ha, what was that?"

The two turned swiftly as a shadow fell across the table. Into the entrance of the cave that formed the bandit lair, a man staggered. His eyes were wide and staring; he reeled on buckling legs, and a dark red stain dyed his tunic. He came a few tottering steps forward, then pitched across the table, sliding off onto the floor.

"Hell's devils!" cursed the Wolf, hauling him upright and propping him in a chair. "Where are the rest, curse you?"

"Dead! All dead!"

"How? Satan's curses on you, speak!" The Wolf shook the man savagely, the other bandit gazing on in wide-eyed horror.

"We reached the hermit's hut just as the moon rose," the man muttered. "I stayed outside — to watch — the others went in — to torture the hermit — to make him reveal — the hiding-place — of his gold."

"Yes, yes! Then what?" The Wolf was raging with impatience.

"Then the world turned red — the hut went up in a roar and a red rain flooded the valley — through it I saw — the hermit and a tall man clad all in black — coming from the trees —"

"Solomon Kane!" gasped the bandit. "I knew it! I —"

"Silence, fool!" snarled the chief. "Go on!"

"I fled — Kane pursued — wounded me — but I outran — him — got — here — first —"

The man slumped forward on the table.

"Saints and devils!" raged the Wolf. "What does he look like, this Kane?"

"Like — Satan —"

The voice trailed off in silence. The dead man slid from the table to lie in a red heap upon the floor.

"Like Satan!" babbled the other bandit. "I told you! 'Tis the Horned One himself! I tell you —"

He ceased as a frightened face peered in at the cave entrance.

"Kane?"

"Aye." The Wolf was too much at sea to lie. "Keep close watch, La Mon; in a moment the Rat and I will join you."

The face withdrew and Le Loup turned to the other.

"This ends the band," said he. "You, I, and that thief La Mon are all that are left. What would you suggest?"

The Rat's pallid lips barely formed the word: "Flight!"

"You are right. Let us take the gems and gold from the chests and flee, using the secret passageway."

"And La Mon?"

"He can watch until we are ready to flee. Then — why divide the treasure three ways?"

A faint smile touched the Rat's malevolent features. Then a sudden thought smote him.

"He," indicating the corpse on the floor, "said, 'I got here first.' Does that mean Kane was pursuing him here?" And as the Wolf nodded impatiently the other turned to the chests with chattering haste.

The flickering candle on the rough table lighted up a strange and wild scene. The light, uncertain and dancing, gleamed redly in the slowly widening lake of blood in which the dead man lay; it danced upon the heaps of gems and coins emptied hastily upon the floor from the brass-bound chests that ranged the walls; and it glittered in the eyes of the Wolf with the same gleam which sparkled from his sheathed dagger.

The chests were empty, their treasure lying in a shimmering mass upon the bloodstained floor. The Wolf stopped and listened. Outside was silence. There was no moon, and Le Loup's keen imagination pictured the dark slayer, Solomon Kane, gliding through the blackness, a shadow among shadows. He grinned crookedly; this time the Englishman would be foiled.

"There is a chest yet unopened," said he, pointing.

The Rat, with a muttered exclamation of surprize, bent over the chest indicated. With a single, catlike motion, the Wolf sprang upon him, sheathing his dagger to the hilt in the Rat's back, between the shoulders. The Rat sagged to the floor without a sound.

"Why divide the treasure two ways?" murmured Le Loup, wiping his blade upon the dead man's doublet. "Now for La Mon."

He stepped toward the door; then stopped and shrank back.

At first he thought that it was the shadow of a man who stood in the entrance; then he saw that it was a man himself, though so dark and still he stood that a fantastic semblance of shadow was lent him by the guttering candle.

A tall man, as tall as Le Loup he was, clad in black from head to foot, in plain, close-fitting garments that somehow suited the somber face. Long arms and broad shoulders betokened the swordsman, as plainly as the long rapier in his hand. The features of the man were saturnine and gloomy. A kind of dark pallor lent him a ghostly appearance in the uncertain light, an effect heightened by the satanic darkness of his lowering brows. Eyes, large, deep-set and unblinking, fixed their gaze upon the bandit, and looking into them, Le Loup was unable to decide what color they were. Strangely, the mephistophelean trend of the lower features was offset by a high, broad forehead, though this was partly hidden by a featherless hat.

That forehead marked the dreamer, the idealist, the introvert, just as the eyes and the thin, straight nose betrayed the fanatic. An observer would have been struck by the eyes of the two men who stood there, facing each other. Eyes of both betokened untold deeps of power, but there the resemblance ceased.

The eyes of the bandit were hard, almost opaque, with a curious scintillant shallowness that reflected a thousand changing lights and gleams, like some strange gem; there was mockery in those eyes, cruelty and recklessness.

The eyes of the man in black, on the other hand, deep-set and staring from under prominent brows, were cold but deep; gazing into them, one had the impression of looking into countless fathoms of ice.

Now the eyes clashed, and the Wolf, who was used to being feared, felt a strange coolness on his spine. The sensation was new to him — a new thrill to one who lived for thrills, and he laughed suddenly.

"You are Solomon Kane, I suppose?" he asked, managing to

make his question sound politely incurious.

"I am Solomon Kane." The voice was resonant and powerful. "Are you prepared to meet your God?"

"Why, *Monsieur*," Le Loup answered, bowing, "I assure you I am as ready as I ever will be. I might ask *Monsieur* the same question."

"No doubt I stated my inquiry wrongly," Kane said grimly. "I will change it: Are you prepared to meet your master, the Devil?"

"As to that, *Monsieur*" — Le Loup examined his finger nails with elaborate unconcern — "I must say that I can at present render a most satisfactory account to his Horned Excellency, though really I have no intention of so doing — for a while at least."

Le Loup did not wonder as to the fate of La Mon; Kane's presence in the cave was sufficient answer that did not need the trace of blood on his rapier to verify it.

"What I wish to know, *Monsieur*," said the bandit, "is why in the Devil's name have you harassed my band as you have, and how did you destroy that last set of fools?"

"Your last question is easily answered, sir," Kane replied. "I myself had the tale spread that the hermit possessed a store of gold, knowing that would draw your scum as carrion draws vultures. For days and nights I have watched the hut, and tonight, when I saw your villains coming, I warned the hermit, and together we went among the trees back of the hut. Then, when the rogues were inside, I struck flint and steel to the train I had laid, and flame ran through the trees like a red snake until it reached the powder I had placed beneath the hut floor. Then the hut and thirteen sinners went to Hell in a great roar of flame and smoke. True, one escaped, but him I had slain in the forest had not I stumbled and fallen upon a broken root, which gave him time to elude me."

"*Monsieur*," said Le Loup with another low bow, "I grant you the admiration I must needs bestow on a brave and shrewd foeman. Yet tell me this: Why have you followed me as a wolf follows deer?"

"Some moons ago," said Kane, his frown becoming more menacing, "you and your fiends raided a small village down the valley. You know the details better than I. There was a girl there, a mere child, who, hoping to escape your lust, fled up the valley; but you, you jackal of Hell, you caught her and left her, violated and dying. I found her there, and above her dead form I made up my mind to hunt you down and kill you."

"H'm," mused the Wolf. "Yes, I remember the wench. *Mon Dieu*, so the softer sentiments enter into the affair! *Monsieur*, I had not thought you an amorous man; be not jealous, good fellow, there are many more wenches."

"Le Loup, take care!" Kane exclaimed, a terrible menace in his voice, "I have never yet done a man to death by torture, but by God, sir, you tempt me!"

The tone, and more especially the unexpected oath, coming as it did from Kane, slightly sobered Le Loup; his eyes narrowed and his hand moved toward his rapier. The air was tense for an instant; then the Wolf relaxed elaborately.

"Who was the girl?" he asked idly. "Your wife?"

"I never saw her before," answered Kane.

"Nom d'un nom!" swore the bandit. "What sort of a man are you, *Monsieur*, who takes up a feud of this sort merely to avenge a wench unknown to you?"

"That, sir, is my own affair; it is sufficient that I do so."

Kane could not have explained, even to himself, nor did he ever seek an explanation within himself. A true fanatic, his promptings were reasons enough for his actions.

"You are right, *Monsieur*." Le Loup was sparring now for time; casually he edged backward inch by inch, with such consummate acting skill that he aroused no suspicion even in the hawk who watched him. *"Monsieur,"* said he, "possibly you will say that you are merely a noble cavalier, wandering about like a true Galahad, protecting the weaker; but you and I know different. There on the floor is the equivalent to an emperor's ransom. Let us divide it peaceably; then if you like not my company, why — *nom d'un nom!* — we can go our separate ways."

Kane leaned forward, a terrible brooding threat growing in his cold eyes. He seemed like a great condor about to launch himself upon his victim.

"Sir, do you assume me to be as great a villain as yourself?"

Suddenly Le Loup threw back his head, his eyes dancing and leaping with a wild mockery and a kind of insane recklessness. His shout of laughter sent the echoes flying.

"Gods of Hell! No, you fool, I do not class you with myself! *Mon Dieu, Monsieur* Kane, you have a task indeed if you intend to avenge all the wenches who have known my favors!"

"Shades of death! Shall I waste time in parleying with this base scoundrel!" Kane snarled in a voice suddenly blood-thirsting, and his lean frame flashed forward like a bent bow suddenly released.

At the same instant Le Loup with a wild laugh bounded backward with a movement as swift as Kane's. His timing was perfect; his back-flung hands struck the table and hurled it aside, plunging the cave into darkness as the candle toppled and went out.

Kane's rapier sang like an arrow in the dark as he thrust blindly and ferociously.

"*Adieu, Monsieur* Galahad!" The taunt came from somewhere in front of him, but Kane, plunging toward the sound with the savage fury of baffled wrath, caromed against a blank wall that did not yield to his blow. From somewhere seemed to come an echo of a mocking laugh.

Kane whirled, eyes fixed on the dimly outlined entrance, thinking his foe would try to slip past him and out of the cave; but no form bulked there, and when his groping hands found the candle and lighted it, the cave was empty, save for himself and the dead men on the floor.

3. The Chant of the Drums

Across the dusky waters the whisper came: boom, boom, boom! — a sullen reiteration. Far away and more faintly sounded a whisper of different timbre: thrum, throom, thrum! Back and forth went the vibrations as the throbbing drums spoke to each other. What tales did they carry? What monstrous secrets whispered across the sullen, shadowy reaches of the unmapped jungle?

"This, you are sure, is the bay where the Spanish ship put in?"

"Yes, *Senhor*, the Negro swears this is the bay where the white man left the ship alone and went into the jungle."

Kane nodded grimly.

"Then put me ashore here, alone. Wait seven days; then if I have not returned and if you have no word of me, set sail wherever you will."

"Yes, *Senhor*."

The waves slapped lazily against the sides of the boat that carried Kane ashore. The village that he sought was on the river bank but set back from the bay shore, the jungle hiding it from sight of the ship.

Kane had adopted what seemed the most hazardous course, that of going ashore by night, for the reason that he knew, if the man he sought were in the village, he would never reach it by day. As it was, he was taking a most desperate chance in daring the nighttime jungle, but all his life he had been used to taking desperate chances. Now he gambled his life upon the slim chance of gaining the Negro village under cover of darkness and unknown to the villagers.

At the beach he left the boat with a few muttered commands, and as the rowers put back to the ship which lay anchored some distance out in the bay, he turned and engulfed himself in the blackness of the jungle. Sword in one hand, dagger in the other, he stole forward, seeking to keep pointed in the direction from which the drums still muttered and grumbled.

He went with the stealth and easy movement of a leopard, feeling his way cautiously, every nerve alert and straining, but the way was not easy. Vines tripped him and slapped him in the face, impeding his progress; he was forced to grope his way between the huge boles of towering trees, and all through the underbrush about him sounded vague and menacing rustlings and shadows of movement. Thrice his foot touched something that moved beneath it and writhed away, and once he glimpsed the baleful glimmer of feline eyes among the trees. They vanished, however, as he advanced.

Thrum, thrum, thrum, came the ceaseless monotone of the drums: war and death (they said); blood and lust; human sacrifice and human feast! The soul of Africa (said the drums); the spirit of the jungle; the chant of the gods of outer darkness, the gods that roar and gibber, the gods men knew when dawns were young, beast-eyed, gaping-mouthed, huge-bellied, bloody-handed, the Black Gods (sang the drums).

All this and more the drums roared and bellowed to Kane as he worked his way through the forest. Somewhere in his soul a responsive chord was smitten and answered. You too are of the night (sang the drums); there is the strength of darkness, the strength of the primitive in you; come back down the ages; let us teach you, let us teach you (chanted the drums).

Kane stepped out of the thick jungle and came upon a plainly defined trail. Beyond through the trees came the gleam of the village fires, flames glowing through the palisades. Kane walked down the trail swiftly.

He went silently and warily, sword extended in front of him, eyes straining to catch any hint of movement in the darkness ahead, for the trees loomed like sullen giants on each hand; sometimes their great branches intertwined above the trail and he could see only a slight way ahead of him.

Like a dark ghost he moved along the shadowed trail; alertly he stared and harkened; yet no warning came first to him, as a great, vague bulk rose up out of the shadows and struck him down, silently.

4. The Black God

Thrum, thrum, thrum! Somewhere, with deadening monotony, a cadence was repeated, over and over, bearing out the same theme: "Fool − fool − fool!" Now it was far away, now he could stretch out his hand and almost reach it. Now it merged with the throbbing in his head until the two vibrations were as one: "Fool − fool − fool − fool −"

The fogs faded and vanished. Kane sought to raise his hand to his head, but found that he was bound hand and foot. He lay on the floor of a hut − alone? He twisted about to view the place. No, two eyes glimmered at him from the darkness. Now a form took shape, and Kane, still mazed, believed that he looked on the man who had struck him unconscious. Yet no; this man could never strike such a blow. He was lean, withered and wrinkled. The only thing that seemed alive about him were his eyes, and they seemed like the eyes of a snake.

The man squatted on the floor of the hut, near the doorway, naked save for a loin-cloth and the usual paraphernalia of bracelets, anklets and armlets. Weird fetishes of ivory, bone and hide, animal and human, adorned his arms and legs. Suddenly and unexpectedly he spoke in English.

"Ha, you wake, white man? Why you come here, eh?"

Kane asked the inevitable question, following the habit of the Caucasian.

"You speak my language − how is that?"

The black man grinned.

"I slave − long time, me boy. Me, N'Longa, ju-ju man, me, great fetish. No black man like me! You white man, you hunt brother?"

Kane snarled. "I! Brother! I seek a man, yes."

The Negro nodded. "Maybe so you find um, eh?"

"He dies!"

Again the Negro grinned. "Me pow'rful ju-ju man," he announced apropos of nothing. He bent closer. "White man you hunt, eyes like a leopard, eh? Yes? Ha! ha! ha! ha! Listen, white man: man-with-eyes-of-a-leopard, he and Chief Songa make pow'rful palaver; they blood brothers now. Say nothing, I help you; you help me, eh?"

"Why should you help me?" asked Kane suspiciously.

The ju-ju man bent closer and whispered, "White man Songa's right-hand man; Songa more pow'rful than N'Longa. White man mighty ju-ju! N'Longa's white brother kill man-with-eyes-of-a-leopard, be blood brother to N'Longa, N'Longa be more pow'rful than Songa; palaver set."

And like a dusky ghost he floated out of the hut so swiftly that Kane was not sure but that the whole affair was a dream.

Without, Kane could see the flare of fires. The drums were still booming, but close at hand the tones merged and mingled, and the impulse-producing vibrations were lost. All seemed a barbaric clamor without rhyme or reason, yet there was an undertone of mockery there, savage and gloating. "Lies," thought Kane, his mind still swimming, "jungle lies like jungle women that lure a man to his doom."

Two warriors entered the hut — black giants, hideous with paint and armed with crude spears. They lifted the white man and carried him out of the hut. They bore him across an open space, leaned him upright against a post and bound him there. About him, behind him and to the side, a great semicircle of black faces leered and faded in the firelight as the flames leaped and sank. There in front of him loomed a shape hideous and obscene — a black, formless thing, a grotesque parody of the human. Still, brooding, bloodstained, like the formless soul of Africa, the horror, the Black God.

And in front and to each side, upon roughly carven thrones of teakwood, sat two men. He who sat upon the right was a black man, huge, ungainly, a gigantic and unlovely mass of dusky flesh and muscles. Small, hoglike eyes blinked out over sin-marked cheeks; huge, flabby red lips pursed in fleshly haughtiness.

The other —

"Ah, *Monsieur*, we meet again." The speaker was far from being the debonair villain who had taunted Kane in the cavern among the mountains. His clothes were rags; there were more lines in his face; he had sunk lower in the years that had passed. Yet his eyes still gleamed and danced with their old recklessness and his voice held the same mocking timbre.

"The last time I heard that accursed voice," said Kane calmly, "was in a cave, in darkness, whence you fled like a hunted rat."

"Aye, under different conditions," answered Le Loup imperturbably. "What did you do after blundering about like an elephant in the dark?"

Kane hesitated, then: "I left the mountain —"

"By the front entrance? Yes? I might have known you were too stupid to find the secret door. Hoofs of the Devil, had you thrust against the chest with the golden lock, which stood against the wall, the door had opened to you and revealed the secret passageway through which I went."

"I traced you to the nearest port and there took ship and followed you to Italy, where I found you had gone."

"Aye, by the saints, you nearly cornered me in Florence. Ho! ho! ho! I was climbing through a back window while *Monsieur* Galahad was battering down the front door of the tavern. And had your horse not gone lame, you would have caught up with me on the road to Rome. Again, the ship on which I left Spain had barely put out to sea when *Monsieur* Galahad rides up to the wharfs. Why have you followed me like this? I do not understand."

"Because you are a rogue whom it is my destiny to kill," answered Kane coldly. He did not understand. All his life he had roamed about the world aiding the weak and fighting oppression, he neither knew nor questioned why. That was his obsession, his driving force of life. Cruelty and tyranny to the weak sent a red blaze of fury, fierce and lasting, through his soul. When the full flame of his hatred was wakened and loosed, there was no rest for him until his vengeance had been fulfilled to the uttermost. If he thought of it at all, he considered himself a fulfiller of God's judgment, a vessel of wrath to be emptied upon the souls of the unrighteous. Yet in the full sense of the word Solomon Kane was not wholly a Puritan, though he thought of himself as such.

Le Loup shrugged his shoulders. "I could understand had I wronged you personally. *Mon Dieu!* I, too, would follow an enemy across the world, but, though I would have joyfully slain and robbed you, I never heard of you until you declared war on me."

Kane was silent, his still fury overcoming him. Though he did not realize it, the Wolf was more than merely an enemy to him; the bandit symbolized, to Kane, all the things against which the Puritan had fought all his life: cruelty, outrage, oppression and tyranny.

Le Loup broke in on his vengeful meditations. "What did you do with the treasure, which — gods of Hades! — took me years to accumulate? Devil take it, I had time only to snatch a handful of coins and trinkets as I ran."

"I took such as I needed to hunt you down. The rest I gave to the villages which you had looted."

"Saints and the devil!" swore Le Loup. "*Monsieur*, you are the greatest fool I have yet met. To throw that vast treasure — by Satan, I rage to think of it in the hands of base peasants, vile villagers! Yet, ho! ho! ho! ho! they will steal, and kill each other for it! That is human nature."

"Yes, damn you!" flamed Kane suddenly, showing that his conscience had not been at rest. "Doubtless they will, being fools. Yet what could I do? Had I left it there, people might have starved and gone naked for lack of it. More, it would have been found, and theft and slaughter would have followed anyway. You are to blame, for had this treasure been left with its rightful owners, no such trouble would have ensued."

The Wolf grinned without reply. Kane not being a profane man, his rare curses had double effect and always startled his hearers, no matter how vicious or hardened they might be.

It was Kane who spoke next. "Why have you fled from me across the world? You do not really fear me."

"No, you are right. Really I do not know; perhaps flight is a habit which is difficult to break. I made my mistake when I did not kill you that night in the mountains. I am sure I could kill you in a fair fight, yet I have never even, ere now, sought to ambush you. Somehow I have not had a liking to meet you, *Monsieur* — a whim of mine, a mere whim. Then — *mon Dieu!* — mayhap I have enjoyed a new sensation — and I had thought that I had exhausted the thrills of life. And then, a man must either be the hunter or the hunted. Until now, *Monsieur*, I was the hunted, but I grew weary of the role — I thought I had thrown you off the trail."

"A Negro slave, brought from this vicinity, told a Portugal ship captain of a white man who landed from a Spanish ship and went into the jungle. I heard of it and hired the ship, paying the captain to bring me here."

"*Monsieur*, I admire you for your attempt, but you must admire me, too! Alone I came into this village, and alone among savages and cannibals I — with some slight knowledge of the language learned from a slave aboard ship — I gained the confidence of King Songa and supplanted that mummer, N'Longa. I am a braver man than you, *Monsieur*, for I had no ship to retreat to, and a ship is waiting for you."

"I admire your courage," said Kane, "but you are content to rule amongst cannibals — you the blackest soul of them all. I intend to return to my own people when I have slain you."

"Your confidence would be admirable were it not amusing. Ho, Gulka!"

A giant Negro stalked into the space between them. He was the hugest man that Kane had ever seen, though he moved with catlike ease and suppleness. His arms and legs were like trees, and the great, sinuous muscles rippled with each motion. His apelike head was set squarely between gigantic shoulders. His great, dusky hands were like the talons of an ape, and his brow slanted back from above bestial eyes. Flat nose and great, thick red lips completed this picture of primitive, lustful savagery.

"That is Gulka, the gorilla-slayer," said Le Loup. "He it was who lay in wait beside the trail and smote you down. You are like a wolf, yourself, *Monsieur* Kane, but since your ship hove in sight you have been watched by many eyes, and had you had all the powers of a leopard, you had not seen Gulka nor heard him. He hunts the most terrible and crafty of all beasts, in their native forests, far to the north, the beasts-who-walk-like-men — as that one, whom he slew some days since."

Kane, following Le Loup's fingers, made out a curious, manlike thing, dangling from a roof-pole of a hut. A jagged end thrust through the thing's body held it there. Kane could scarcely distinguish its characteristics by the firelight, but there was a weird, humanlike semblance about the hideous, hairy thing.

"A female gorilla that Gulka slew and brought to the village," said Le Loup.

The giant black slouched close to Kane and stared into the white man's eyes. Kane returned his gaze somberly, and presently the Negro's eyes dropped sullenly and he slouched back a few paces. The look in the Puritan's grim eyes had pierced the primitive hazes of the gorilla-slayer's soul, and for the first time in his life he felt fear. To throw this off, he tossed a challenging look about; then, with unexpected animalness, he struck his huge chest resoundingly, grinned cavernously and flexed his mighty arms. No one spoke. Primordial bestiality had the stage, and the more highly developed types looked on with various feelings of amusement, tolerance or contempt.

Gulka glanced furtively at Kane to see if the white man was watching him, then with a sudden beastly roar, plunged forward and dragged a man from the semicircle. While the trembling victim screeched for mercy, the giant hurled him upon the crude altar before the shadowy idol. A spear rose and flashed, and the screeching ceased. The Black God looked on, his monstrous features seeming to leer in the flickering firelight. He had drunk; was the Black God pleased with the draft — with the sacrifice?

Gulka stalked back, and stopping before Kane, flourished the bloody spear before the white man's face.

Le Loup laughed. Then suddenly N'Longa appeared. He came from nowhere in particular; suddenly he was standing there, beside the post to which Kane was bound. A lifetime of study of the art of illusion had given the ju-ju man a highly technical knowledge of appearing and disappearing — which after all, consisted only in timing the audience's attention.

He waved Gulka aside with a grand gesture, and the gorilla-man slunk back, apparently to get out of N'Longa's gaze — then with incredible swiftness he turned and struck the ju-ju man a terrific blow upon the side of the head with his open hand. N'Longa went down like a felled ox, and in an instant he had been seized and bound to a post close to Kane. An uncertain murmuring rose from the Negroes, which died out as King Songa stared angrily toward them.

Le Loup leaned back upon his throne and laughed uproariously.

"The trail ends here, *Monsieur* Galahad. That ancient fool thought I did not know of his plotting! I was hiding outside the hut and heard the interesting conversation you two had. Ha! ha! ha! ha! The Black God must drink, *Monsieur*, but I have persuaded Songa to have you two burnt; that will be much more enjoyable, though we shall have to forego the usual feast, I fear. For after the fires are lit about your feet the devil himself could not keep your carcasses from becoming charred frames of bone."

Songa shouted something imperiously, and blacks came bearing wood, which they piled about the feet of N'Longa and Kane. The ju-ju man had recovered consciousness, and he now shouted something in his native language. Again the murmuring arose among the shadowy throng. Songa snarled something in reply.

Kane gazed at the scene almost impersonally. Again, somewhere in his soul, dim primal deeps were stirring, age-old thought memories, veiled in the fogs of lost eons. He had been here before, thought Kane; he knew all this of old — the lurid flames beating back the sullen night, the bestial faces leering expectantly, and the god, the Black God, there in the shadows! Always the Black God, brooding back in the shadows. He had known the shouts, the frenzied chant of the worshipers, back there in the gray dawn of the world, the speech of the bellowing drums, the singing priests, the repellent, inflaming, all-pervading scent of freshly spilt blood. All this have I known, somewhere, sometime, thought Kane; now I am the main actor —

He became aware that someone was speaking to him through the roar of the drums; he had not realized that the drums had begun to boom again. The speaker was N'Longa:

"Me pow'rful ju-ju man! Watch now: I work mighty magic. Songa!" His voice rose in a screech that drowned out the wildly clamoring drums.

Songa grinned at the words N'Longa screamed at him. The chant of the drums now had dropped to a low, sinister monotone and Kane plainly heard Le Loup when he spoke:

"N'Longa says that he will now work that magic which it is death to speak, even. Never before has it been worked in the sight of living men; it is the nameless ju-ju magic. Watch closely, *Monsieur*, possibly we shall be further amused." The Wolf laughed lightly and sardonically.

A black man stooped, applying a torch to the wood about Kane's feet. Tiny jets of flame began to leap up and catch. Another bent to do the same with N'Longa, then hesitated. The ju-ju man sagged in his bonds; his head drooped upon his chest. He seemed dying.

Le Loup leaned forward, cursing, "Feet of the Devil! Is the scoundrel about to cheat us of our pleasure of seeing him writhe in the flames?"

The warrior gingerly touched the wizard and said something in his own language.

Le Loup laughed: "He died of fright. A great wizard, by the —"

His voice trailed off suddenly. The drums stopped as if the drummers had fallen dead simultaneously. Silence dropped like a fog upon the village and in the stillness Kane heard only the sharp crackle of the flames whose heat he was beginning to feel.

All eyes were turned upon the dead man upon the altar, *for the corpse had begun to move!*

First a twitching of a hand, then an aimless motion of an arm, a motion which gradually spread over the body and limbs. Slowly, with blind, uncertain gestures, the dead man turned upon his side, the trailing limbs found the earth. Then, horribly like something being born, like some frightful reptilian thing bursting the shell of non-existence, the corpse tottered and reared upright, standing on legs wide apart and stiffly braced, arms still making useless, infantile motions. Utter silence, save somewhere a man's quick breath sounded loud in the stillness.

Kane stared, for the first time in his life smitten speechless and thoughtless. To his Puritan mind this was Satan's hand manifested.

Le Loup sat on his throne, eyes wide and staring, hand still half-raised in the careless gesture he was making when frozen into silence by the unbelievable sight. Songa sat beside him, mouth and eyes wide open, fingers making curious jerky motions upon the carved arms of the throne.

Now the corpse was upright, swaying on stiltlike legs, body tilting far back until the sightless eyes seemed to stare straight into the red moon that was just rising over the black jungle. The thing tottered uncertainly in a wide, erratic half-circle, arms flung out grotesquely as if in balance, then swayed about to face the two thrones — and the Black God. A burning twig at Kane's feet cracked like the crash of a cannon in the tense silence. The horror thrust forth a black foot — it took a wavering step — another. Then with stiff, jerky and automatonlike steps, legs straddled far apart, the dead man came toward the two who sat in speechless horror to each side of the Black God.

"Ah-h-h!" from somewhere came the explosive sigh, from that shadowy semicircle where crouched the terror-fascinated worshipers. Straight on stalked the grim specter. Now it was within three strides of the thrones, and Le Loup, faced by fear for the first time in his bloody life, cringed back in his chair; while Songa, with a superhuman effort breaking the chains of horror that held him helpless, shattered the night with a wild scream and, springing to his feet, lifted a spear, shrieking and gibbering in wild menace. Then as the ghastly thing halted not its frightful advance, he hurled the spear with all the power of his great, black muscles, and the spear tore through the dead man's breast with a rending of flesh and bone. Not an instant halted the thing — for the dead die not — and Songa the king stood frozen, arms outstretched as if to fend off the terror.

An instant they stood so, leaping firelight and eery moonlight etching the scene forever in the minds of the beholders. The changeless staring eyes of the corpse looked full into the bulging eyes of Songa, where were reflected all the hells of horror. Then with a jerky motion the arms of the thing went out and up. The dead hands fell on Songa's shoulders. At the first touch, the king seemed to shrink and shrivel, and with a scream that was to haunt the dreams of every watcher through all the rest of time, Songa crumpled and fell, and the dead man reeled stiffly and fell with him. Motionless lay the two at the feet of the Black God, and to Kane's dazed mind it seemed that the idol's great, inhuman eyes were fixed upon them with terrible, still laughter.

At the instant of the king's fall, a great shout went up from the blacks, and Kane, with a clarity lent his subconscious mind by the depths of his hate, looked for Le Loup and saw him spring from his throne and vanish in the darkness. Then vision was blurred by a rush of black figures who swept into the space before the god. Feet knocked aside the blazing brands whose heat Kane had forgotten, and dusky hands freed him; others loosed the wizard's body and laid it upon the earth. Kane dimly understood that the blacks believed this thing to be the work of N'Longa, and that they connected the vengeance of the wizard with himself. He bent, laid a hand on the ju-ju man's shoulder. No doubt of it: he was dead, the flesh was already cold. He glanced at the other corpses. Songa was dead, too, and the thing that had slain him lay now without movement.

Kane started to rise, then halted. Was he dreaming, or did he really feel a sudden warmth in the dead flesh he touched? Mind reeling, he again bent over the wizard's body, and slowly he felt warmness steal over the limbs and the blood begin to flow sluggishly through the veins again.

Then N'Longa opened his eyes and stared up into Kane's, with the blank expression of a new-born babe. Kane watched, flesh crawling, and saw the knowing, reptilian glitter come back, saw the wizard's thick lips part in a wide grin. N'Longa sat up, and a strange chant arose from the Negroes.

Kane looked about. The blacks were all kneeling, swaying their bodies to and fro, and in their shouts Kane caught the word, "N'Longa!" repeated over and over in a kind of fearsomely ecstatic refrain of terror and worship. As the wizard rose, they all fell prostrate.

N'Longa nodded, as if in satisfaction.

"Great ju-ju — great fetish, me!" he announced to Kane. "You see? My ghost go out — kill Songa — come back to me! Great magic! Great fetish, me!"

Kane glanced at the Black God looming back in the shadows, at N'Longa, who now flung out his arms toward the idol as if in invocation.

I am everlasting (Kane thought the Black God said); I drink, no matter who rules; chiefs, slayers, wizards, they pass like the ghosts of dead men through the gray jungle; I stand, I rule; I am the soul of the jungle (said the Black God).

Suddenly Kane came back from the illusory mists in which he had been wandering. "The white man! Which way did he flee?"

N'Longa shouted something. A score of dusky hands pointed; from somewhere Kane's rapier was thrust out to him. The fogs faded and vanished; again he was the avenger, the scourge of the unrighteous; with the sudden volcanic speed of a tiger he snatched the sword and was gone.

5. The End of the Red Trail

Limbs and vines slapped against Kane's face. The oppressive steam of the tropic night rose like mist about him. The moon, now floating high above the jungle, limned the black shadows in its white glow and patterned the jungle floor in grotesque designs. Kane knew not if the man he sought was ahead of him, but broken limbs and trampled underbrush showed that some man had gone that way, some man who fled in haste, nor halted to pick his way. Kane followed these signs unswervingly. Believing in the justice of his vengeance, he did not doubt that the dim beings who rule men's destinies would finally bring him face to face with Le Loup.

Behind him the drums boomed and muttered. What a tale they had to tell this night of the triumph of N'Longa, the death of the black king, the overthrow of the white-man-with-eyes-like-a-leopard, and a more darksome tale, a tale to be whispered in low, muttering vibrations: the nameless ju-ju.

Was he dreaming? Kane wondered as he hurried on. Was all this part of some foul magic? He had seen a dead man rise and slay and die again; he had seen a man die and come to life again. Did N'Longa in truth send his ghost, his soul, his life essence forth into the void, dominating a corpse to do his will? Aye, N'Longa died a real death there, bound to the torture stake, and he who lay dead on the altar rose and did as N'Longa would have done had he been free. Then, the unseen force animating the dead man fading, N'Longa had lived again.

Yes, Kane thought, he must admit it as a fact. Somewhere in the darksome reaches of jungle and river, N'Longa had stumbled upon the Secret — the Secret of controlling life and death, of overcoming the shackles and limitations of the flesh. How had this dark wisdom, born in the black and blood-stained shadows of this grim land, been given to the wizard? What sacrifice had been so pleasing to the Black Gods, what ritual so monstrous, as to make them give up the knowledge of this magic? And what thoughtless, timeless journeys had N'Longa taken, when he chose to send his ego, his ghost, through the far, misty countries, reached only by death?

There is wisdom in the shadows (brooded the drums), wisdom and magic; go into the darkness for wisdom; ancient magic shuns the light; we remember the lost ages (whispered the drums), ere man became wise and foolish; we remember the beast gods — the serpent gods and the ape gods and the nameless, the Black Gods, they who drank blood and whose voices roared through the shadowy hills, who feasted and lusted. The secrets of life and of death are theirs; we remember, we remember (sang the drums).

Kane heard them as he hastened on. The tale they told to the feathered black warriors farther up the river, he could not translate; but they spoke to him in their own way, and that language was deeper, more basic.

The moon, high in the dark blue skies, lighted his way and gave him a clear vision as he came out at last into a glade and saw Le Loup standing there. The Wolf's naked blade was a long gleam of silver in the moon, and he stood with shoulders thrown back, the old, defiant smile still on his face.

"A long trail, *Monsieur*," said he. "It began in the mountains of France; it ends in an African jungle. I have wearied of the game at last, *Monsieur* — and you die. I had not fled from the village, even, save that — I admit it freely — that damnable witchcraft of N'Longa's shook my nerves. More, I saw that the whole tribe would turn against me."

Kane advanced warily, wondering what dim, forgotten tinge of chivalry in the bandit's soul had caused him thus to take his chance in the open. He half-suspected treachery, but his keen eyes could detect no shadow of movement in the jungle on either side of the glade.

"*Monsieur*, on guard!" Le Loup's voice was crisp. "Time that we ended this fool's dance about the world. Here we are alone."

The men were now within reach of each other, and Le Loup, in the midst of his sentence, suddenly plunged forward with the speed of light, thrusting viciously. A slower man had died there, but Kane parried and sent his own blade in a silver streak that slit Le Loup's tunic as the Wolf bounded backward. Le Loup admitted the failure of his trick with a wild laugh and came in with the breath-taking speed and fury of a tiger, his blade making a white fan of steel about him.

Rapier clashed on rapier as the two swordsmen fought. They were fire and ice opposed. Le Loup fought wildly but craftily, leaving no openings, taking advantage of every opportunity. He was a living flame, bounding back, leaping in, feinting, thrusting, warding, striking — laughing like a wild man, taunting and cursing.

Kane's skill was cold, calculating, scintillant. He made no waste movement, no motion not absolutely necessary. He seemed to devote more time and effort toward defense than did Le Loup, yet there was no hesitancy in his attack, and when he thrust, his blade shot out with the speed of a striking snake.

There was little to choose between the men as to height, strength and reach. Le Loup was the swifter by a scant, flashing margin, but Kane's skill reached a finer point of perfection. The Wolf's fencing was fiery, dynamic, like the blast from a furnace. Kane was more steady — less the instinctive, more the thinking fighter, though he, too, was a born slayer, with the coordination that only a natural fighter possessed.

Thrust, parry, a feint, a sudden whirl of blades —

"Ha!" the Wolf sent up a shout of ferocious laughter as the blood started from a cut on Kane's cheek. As if the sight drove him to further fury, he attacked like the beast men named him. Kane was forced back before that blood-lusting onslaught, but the Puritan's expression did not alter.

Minutes flew by; the clang and clash of steel did not diminish. Now they stood squarely in the center of the glade, Le Loup untouched, Kane's garments red with the blood that oozed from wounds on cheek, breast, arm and thigh. The Wolf grinned savagely and mockingly in the moonlight, but he had begun to doubt.

His breath came hissing fast and his arm began to weary; who was this man of steel and ice who never seemed to weaken? Le Loup knew that the wounds he had inflicted on Kane were not deep, but even so, the steady flow of blood should have sapped some of the man's strength and speed by this time. But if Kane felt the ebb of his powers, it did not show. His brooding countenance did not change in expression, and he pressed the fight with as much cold fury as at the beginning.

Le Loup felt his might fading, and with one last desperate effort he rallied all his fury and strength into a single plunge. A sudden, unexpected attack too wild and swift for the eye to follow, a dynamic burst of speed and fury no man could have withstood, and Solomon Kane reeled for the first time as he felt cold steel tear through his body. He reeled back, and Le Loup, with a wild shout, plunged after him, his reddened sword free, a gasping taunt on his lips.

Kane's sword, backed by the force of desperation, met Le Loup's in midair; met, held and wrenched. The Wolf's yell of triumph died on his lips as his sword flew singing from his hand.

For a fleeting instant he stopped short, arms flung wide as a crucifix, and Kane heard his wild, mocking laughter peal forth for the last time, as the Englishman's rapier made a silver line in the moonlight.

Far away came the mutter of the drums. Kane mechanically cleansed his sword on his tattered garments. The trail ended here, and Kane was conscious of a strange feeling of futility. He always felt that, after he had killed a foe. Somehow it always seemed that no real good had been wrought; as if the foe had, after all, escaped his just vengeance.

With a shrug of his shoulders Kane turned his attention to his bodily needs. Now that the heat of battle had passed, he began to feel weak and faint from the loss of blood. That last thrust had been close; had he not managed to avoid its full point by a twist of his body, the blade had transfixed him. As it was, the sword had struck glancingly, plowed along his ribs and sunk deep in the muscles beneath the shoulder blade, inflicting a long, shallow wound.

Kane looked about him and saw that a small stream trickled through the glade at the far side. Here he made the only mistake of that kind that he ever made in his entire life. Mayhap he was dizzy from loss of blood and still mazed from the weird happenings of the night; be that as it may, he laid down his rapier and crossed, weaponless, to the stream. There he laved his wounds and bandaged them as best he could, with strips torn from his clothing.

Then he rose and was about to retrace his steps when a motion among the trees on the side of the glade where he first entered, caught his eye. A huge figure stepped out of the jungle, and Kane saw, and recognized, his doom. The man was Gulka, the gorilla-slayer. Kane remembered that he had not seen the black among those doing homage to N'Longa. How could he know the craft and hatred in that dusky, slanting skull that had led the Negro, escaping the vengeance of his tribesmen, to trail down the only man he had ever feared? The Black God had been kind to his neophyte; had led him upon his victim helpless and unarmed. Now Gulka could kill his man openly — and slowly, as a leopard kills, not smiting him down from ambush as he had planned, silently and suddenly.

A wide grin split the Negro's face, and he moistened his lips. Kane, watching him, was coldly and deliberately weighing his chances. Gulka had already spied the rapiers. He was closer to them than was Kane. The Englishman knew that there was no chance of his winning in a sudden race for the swords.

A slow, deadly rage surged in him — the fury of helplessness. The blood churned in his temples and his eyes smoldered with a terrible light as he eyed the Negro. His fingers spread and closed like claws. They were strong, those hands; men had died in their clutch. Even Gulka's huge black column of a neck might break like a rotten branch between them — a wave of weakness made the futility of these thoughts apparent to an extent that needed not the verification of the moonlight glimmering from the spear in Gulka's black hand. Kane could not even have fled had he wished — and he had never fled from a single foe.

The gorilla-slayer moved out into the glade. Massive, terrible, he was the personification of the primitive, the Stone Age. His mouth yawned in a red cavern of a grin; he bore himself with the haughty arrogance of savage might.

Kane tensed himself for the struggle that could end but one way. He strove to rally his waning forces. Useless; he had lost too much blood. At least he would meet his death on his feet, and somehow he stiffened his buckling knees and held himself erect, though the glade shimmered before him in uncertain waves and the moon-light seemed to have become a red fog through which he dimly glimpsed the approaching black man.

Kane stooped, though the effort nearly pitched him on his face; he dipped water in his cupped hands and dashed it into his face. This revived him, and he straightened, hoping that Gulka would charge and get it over with before his weakness crumpled him to the earth.

Gulka was now about the center of the glade, moving with the slow, easy stride of a great cat stalking a victim. He was not at all in a hurry to consummate his purpose. He wanted to toy with his victim, to see fear come into those grim eyes which had looked him down, even when the possessor of those eyes had been bound to the death stake. He wanted to slay, at last, slowly, glutting his tigerish blood-lust and torture-lust to the fullest extent.

Then suddenly he halted, turned swiftly, facing another side of the glade. Kane, wondering, followed his glance.

At first it seemed like a blacker shadow among the jungle shadows. At first there was no motion, no sound, but Kane instinctively knew that some terrible menace lurked there in the darkness that masked and merged the silent trees. A sullen horror brooded there, and Kane felt as if, from that monstrous shadow, inhuman eyes seared his very soul. Yet simultaneously there came the fantastic sensation that these eyes were not directed on him. He looked at the gorilla-slayer.

The black man had apparently forgotten him; he stood, half-crouching, spear lifted, eyes fixed upon that clump of blackness. Kane looked again. Now there was motion in the shadows; they merged fantastically and moved out into the glade, much as Gulka had done. Kane blinked: was this the illusion that precedes death?

The shape he looked upon was such as he had visioned dimly in wild nightmares, when the wings of sleep bore him back through lost ages.

He thought at first it was some blasphemous mockery of a man, for it went erect and was tall as a tall man. But it was inhumanly broad and thick, and its gigantic arms hung nearly to its misshapen feet. Then the moonlight smote full upon its bestial face, and Kane's mazed mind thought that the thing was the Black God coming out of the shadows, animated and blood-lusting. Then he saw that it was covered with hair, and he remembered the manlike thing dangling from the roof-pole in the native village. He looked at Gulka.

The Negro was facing the gorilla, spear at the charge. He was not afraid, but his sluggish mind was wondering over the miracle that brought this beast so far from his native jungles.

The mighty ape came out into the moonlight and there was a terrible majesty about his movements. He was nearer Kane than Gulka but he did not seem to be aware of the white man. His small, blazing eyes were fixed on the black man with terrible intensity. He advanced with a curious swaying stride.

Far away the drums whispered through the night, like an accompaniment to this grim Stone Age drama. The savage crouched in the middle of the glade, but the primordial came out of the jungle with eyes bloodshot and blood-lusting. The Negro was face to face with a thing more primitive than he. Again ghosts of memories whispered to Kane: you have seen such sights before (they murmured), back in the dim days, the dawn days, when beast and beast-man battled for supremacy.

Gulka moved away from the ape in a half-circle, crouching, spear ready. With all his craft he was seeking to trick the gorilla, to make a swift kill, for he had never before met such a monster as this, and though he did not fear, he had begun to doubt. The ape made no attempt to stalk or circle; he strode straight forward toward Gulka.

The black man who faced him and the white man who watched could not know the brutish love, the brutish hate that had driven the monster down from the low, forest-covered hills of the north to follow for leagues the trail of him who was the scourge of his kind — the slayer of his mate, whose body now hung from the roof-pole of the Negro village.

The end came swiftly, almost like a sudden gesture. They were close, now, beast and beast-man; and suddenly, with an earth-shaking roar, the gorilla charged. A great hairy arm smote aside the thrusting spear, and the ape closed with the Negro. There was a shattering sound as of many branches breaking simultaneously, and Gulka slumped silently to the earth, to lie with arms, legs and body flung in strange, unnatural positions. The ape towered an instant above him, like a statue of the primordial triumphant.

Far away Kane heard the drums murmur. The soul of the jungle, the soul of the jungle: this phrase surged through his mind with monotonous reiteration.

The three who had stood in power before the Black God that night, where were they? Back in the village where the drums rustled lay Songa — King Songa, once lord of life and death, now a shriveled corpse with a face set in a mask of horror. Stretched on his back in the middle of the glade lay he whom Kane had followed many a league by land and sea. And Gulka the gorilla-slayer lay at the feet of his killer, broken at last by the savagery which had made him a true son of this grim land which had at last overwhelmed him.

Yet the Black God still reigned, thought Kane dizzily, brooding back in the shadows of this dark country, bestial, blood-lusting, caring naught who lived or died, so that he drank.

Kane watched the mighty ape, wondering how long it would be before the huge simian spied and charged him. But the gorilla gave no evidence of having even seen him. Some dim impulse of vengeance yet unglutted prompting him, he bent and raised the Negro. Then he slouched toward the jungle, Gulka's limbs trailing limply and grotesquely. As he reached the trees, the ape halted, whirling the giant form high in the air with seemingly no effort, and dashed the dead man up among the branches. There was a rending sound as a broken projecting limb tore through the body hurled so powerfully against it, and the dead gorilla-slayer dangled there hideously.

A moment the clear moon limned the great ape in its glimmer, as he stood silently gazing up at his victim; then like a dark shadow he melted noiselessly into the jungle.

Kane walked slowly to the middle of the glade and took up his rapier. The blood had ceased to flow from his wounds, and some of his strength was returning, enough, at least, for him to reach the coast where his ship awaited him. He halted at the edge of the glade for a backward glance at Le Loup's upturned face and still form, white in the moonlight, and at the dark shadow among the trees that was Gulka, left by some bestial whim, hanging as the she-gorilla hung in the village.

Afar the drums muttered: "The wisdom of our land is ancient; the wisdom of our land is dark; whom we serve, we destroy. Flee if you would live, but you will never forget our chant. Never, never," sang the drums.

Kane turned to the trail which led to the beach and the ship waiting there.

THE HARP OF ALFRED

Weird Tales, September 1928

I heard the harp of Alfred
  As I went o'er the downs,
When thorn-trees stood at even
  Like monks in dusky gowns;
I heard the music Guthrum heard
  Beside the wasted towns;

When Alfred, like a peasant,
  Came harping down the hill,
  And the drunken Danes made merry
With the man they sought to kill,
  And the Saxon king laughed in their beards
  And bent them to his will.

I heard the harp of Alfred
  As twilight waned to night;
I heard ghost armies tramping
  As the dim stars flamed white;
And Guthrum walked at my left hand,
  And Alfred at my right.

EASTER ISLAND

Weird Tales, December 1928

How many weary centuries have flown
Since strange-eyed beings walked this ancient shore;
Hearing, as we, the green Pacific's roar,
Hewing fantastic gods from sullen stone!
The sands are bare; the idols stand alone.
Impotent 'gainst the years was all their lore:
They are forgot in ages dim and hoar;
Yet still, as then, the long tide-surges drone.

What dreams had they, that shaped these uncouth things?
Before these gods what victims bled and died?
What purple galleys swept along the strand
That bore the tribute of what dim sea-kings?
But now they reign o'er a forgotten land,
Gazing forever out beyond the tide.

SKULLS IN THE STARS

Weird Tales, January 1929

> He told how murderers walk the earth
> Beneath the curse of Cain,
> With crimson clouds before their eyes
> And flames about their brain:
> For blood has left upon their souls
> Its everlasting stain.
>
> — Hood

1

There are two roads to Torkertown. One, the shorter and more direct route, leads across a barren upland moor, and the other, which is much longer, winds its tortuous way in and out among the hummocks and quagmires of the swamps, skirting the low hills to the east. It was a dangerous and tedious trail; so Solomon Kane halted in amazement when a breathless youth from the village he had just left, overtook him and implored him for God's sake to take the swamp road.

"The swamp road!" Kane stared at the boy.

He was a tall, gaunt man, was Solomon Kane, his darkly pallid face and deep brooding eyes made more somber by the drab Puritanical garb he affected.

"Yes, sir, 'tis far safer," the youngster answered his surprized exclamation.

"Then the moor road must be haunted by Satan himself, for your townsmen warned me against traversing the other."

"Because of the quagmires, sir, that you might not see in the dark. You had better return to the village and continue your journey in the morning, sir."

"Taking the swamp road?"

"Yes, sir."

Kane shrugged his shoulders and shook his head.

"The moon rises almost as soon as twilight dies. By its light I can reach Torkertown in a few hours, across the moor."

"Sir, you had better not. No one ever goes that way. There are no houses at all upon the moor, while in the swamp there is the house of old Ezra who lives there all alone since his maniac cousin, Gideon, wandered off and died in the swamp and was never found — and old Ezra though a miser would not refuse you lodging should you decide to stop until morning. Since you must go, you had better go the swamp road."

Kane eyed the boy piercingly. The lad squirmed and shuffled his feet.

"Since this moor road is so dour to wayfarers," said the Puritan, "why did not the villagers tell me the whole tale, instead of vague mouthings?"

"Men like not to talk of it, sir. We hoped that you would take the swamp road after the men advised you to, but when we watched and saw that you turned not at the forks, they sent me to run after you and beg you to reconsider."

"Name of the Devil!" exclaimed Kane sharply, the unaccustomed oath showing his irritation; "the swamp road and the moor road — what is it that threatens me and why should I go miles out of my way and risk the bogs and mires?"

"Sir," said the boy, dropping his voice and drawing closer, "we be simple villagers who like not to talk of such things lest foul fortune befall us, but the moor road is a way accurst and hath not been traversed by any of the countryside for a year or more. It is death to walk those moors by night, as hath been found by some score of unfortunates. Some foul horror haunts the way and claims men for his victims."

"So? And what is this thing like?"

"No man knows. None has ever seen it and lived, but late-farers have heard terrible laughter far out on the fen and men have heard the horrid shrieks of its victims. Sir, in God's name return to the village, there pass the night, and tomorrow take the swamp trail to Torkertown."

Far back in Kane's gloomy eyes a scintillant light had begun to glimmer, like a witch's torch glinting under fathoms of cold gray ice. His blood quickened. Adventure! The lure of life-risk and battle! The thrill of breathtaking, touch-and-go drama! Not that Kane recognized his sensations as such. He sincerely considered that he voiced his real feelings when he said:

"These things be deeds of some power of evil. The lords of darkness have laid a curse upon the country. A strong man is needed to combat Satan and his might. Therefore I go, who have defied him many a time."

"Sir," the boy began, then closed his mouth as he saw the futility of argument. He only added, "The corpses of the victims are bruised and torn, sir."

He stood there at the crossroads, sighing regretfully as he watched the tall, rangy figure swinging up the road that led toward the moors.

The sun was setting as Kane came over the brow of the low hill which debouched into the upland fen. Huge and blood-red it sank down behind the sullen horizon of the moors, seeming to touch the rank grass with fire; so for a moment the watcher seemed to be gazing out across a sea of blood. Then the dark shadows came gliding from the east, the western blaze faded, and Solomon Kane struck out boldly in the gathering darkness.

The road was dim from disuse but was clearly defined. Kane went swiftly but warily, sword and pistols at hand. Stars blinked out and night winds whispered among the grass like weeping specters. The moon began to rise, lean and haggard, like a skull among the stars.

Then suddenly Kane stopped short. From somewhere in front of him sounded a strange and eerie echo — or something like an echo. Again, this time louder. Kane started forward again. Were his senses deceiving him? No!

Far out, there pealed a whisper of frightful laughter. And again, closer this time. No human being ever laughed like that — there was no mirth in it, only hatred and horror and soul-destroying terror. Kane halted. He was not afraid, but for the second he was almost unnerved. Then, stabbing through that awesome laughter, came the sound of a scream that was undoubtedly human. Kane started forward, increasing his gait. He cursed the illusive lights and flickering shadows which veiled the moor in the rising moon and made accurate sight impossible. The laughter continued, growing louder, as did the screams. Then sounded faintly the drum of frantic human feet. Kane broke into a run.

Some human was being hunted to his death out there on the fen, and by what manner of horror God alone knew. The sound of the flying feet halted abruptly and the screaming rose unbearably, mingled with other sounds unnamable and hideous. Evidently the man had been overtaken, and Kane, his flesh crawling, visualized some ghastly fiend of the darkness crouching on the back of its victim — crouching and tearing.

Then the noise of a terrible and short struggle came clearly through the abysmal silence of the fen and the footfalls began again, but stumbling and uneven. The screaming continued, but with a gasping gurgle. The sweat stood cold on Kane's forehead and body. This was heaping horror on horror in an intolerable manner.

God, for a moment's clear light! The frightful drama was being enacted within a very short distance of him, to judge by the ease with which the sounds reached him. But this hellish half-light veiled all in shifting shadows, so that the moors appeared a haze of blurred illusions, and stunted trees and bushes seemed like giants.

Kane shouted, striving to increase the speed of his advance. The shrieks of the unknown broke into a hideous shrill squealing; again there was the sound of a struggle, and then from the shadows of the tall grass a thing came reeling — a thing that had once been a man — a gore-covered, frightful thing that fell at Kane's feet and writhed and groveled and raised its terrible face to the rising moon, and gibbered and yammered, and fell down again and died in its own blood.

The moon was up now and the light was better. Kane bent above the body, which lay stark in its unnamable mutilation, and he shuddered — a rare thing for him, who had seen the deeds of the Spanish Inquisition and the witch-finders.

Some wayfarer, he supposed. Then like a hand of ice on his spine he was aware that he was not alone. He looked up, his cold eyes piercing the shadows whence the dead man had staggered. He saw nothing, but he knew — he felt — that other eyes gave back his stare, terrible eyes not of this earth. He straightened and drew a pistol, waiting. The moonlight spread like a lake of pale blood over the moor, and trees and grasses took on their proper sizes.

The shadows melted, and Kane *saw!* At first he thought it only a shadow of mist, a wisp of moor fog that swayed in the tall grass before him. He gazed. More illusion, he thought. Then the thing began to take on shape, vague and indistinct. Two hideous eyes flamed at him — eyes which held all the stark horror which has been the heritage of man since the fearful dawn ages — eyes frightful and insane, with an insanity transcending earthly insanity. The form of the thing was misty and vague, a brain-shattering travesty on the human form, like, yet horridly unlike. The grass and bushes beyond showed clearly through it.

Kane felt the blood pound in his temples, yet he was as cold as ice. How such an unstable being as that which wavered before him could harm a man in a physical way was more than he could understand, yet the red horror at his feet gave mute testimony that the fiend could act with terrible material effect.

Of one thing Kane was sure: there would be no hunting of him across the dreary moors, no screaming and fleeing to be dragged down again and again. If he must die he would die in his tracks, his wounds in front.

Now a vague and grisly mouth gaped wide and the demoniac laughter again shrieked out, soul-shaking in its nearness. And in the midst of that threat of doom, Kane deliberately leveled his long pistol and fired. A maniacal yell of rage and mockery answered the report, and the thing came at him like a flying sheet of smoke, long shadowy arms stretched to drag him down.

Kane, moving with the dynamic speed of a famished wolf, fired the second pistol with as little effect, snatched his long rapier from its sheath and thrust into the center of the misty attacker. The blade sang as it passed clear through, encountering no solid resistance, and Kane felt icy fingers grip his limbs, bestial talons tear his garments and the skin beneath.

He dropped the useless sword and sought to grapple with his foe. It was like fighting a floating mist, a flying shadow armed with daggerlike claws. His savage blows met empty air, his leanly mighty arms, in whose grasp strong men had died, swept nothingness and clutched emptiness. Naught was solid or real save the flaying, ape-like fingers with their crooked talons, and the crazy eyes which burned into the shuddering depths of his soul.

Kane realized that he was in a desperate plight indeed. Already his garments hung in tatters and he bled from a score of deep wounds. But he never flinched, and the thought of flight never entered his mind. He had never fled from a single foe, and had the thought occurred to him he would have flushed with shame.

He saw no help for it now, but that his form should lie there beside the fragments of the other victim, but the thought held no terrors for him. His only wish was to give as good an account of himself as possible before the end came, and if he could, to inflict some damage on his unearthly foe.

There above the dead man's torn body, man fought with demon

under the pale light of the rising moon, with all the advantages with the demon, save one. And that one was enough to overcome all the others. For if abstract hate may bring into material substance a ghostly thing, may not courage, equally abstract, form a concrete weapon to combat that ghost?

Kane fought with his arms and his feet and his hands, and he was aware at last that the ghost began to give back before him, that the fearful laughter changed to screams of baffled fury. For man's only weapon is courage that flinches not from the gates of Hell itself, and against such not even the legions of Hell can stand.

Of this Kane knew nothing; he only knew that the talons which tore and rended him seemed to grow weaker and wavering, that a wild light grew and grew in the horrible eyes. And reeling and gasping, he rushed in, grappled the thing at last and threw it, and as they tumbled about on the moor and it writhed and lapped his limbs like a serpent of smoke, his flesh crawled and his hair stood on end, for he began to understand its gibbering.

He did not hear and comprehend as a man hears and comprehends the speech of a man, but the frightful secrets it imparted in whisperings and yammerings and screaming silences sank fingers of ice and flame into his soul, and he *knew*.

2

The hut of old Ezra the miser stood by the road in the midst of the swamp, half-screened by the sullen trees which grew about it. The walls were rotting, the roof crumbling, and great, pallid and green fungus-monsters clung to it and writhed about the doors and windows, as if seeking to peer within. The trees leaned above it and their gray branches intertwined so that it crouched in the semi-darkness like a monstrous dwarf over whose shoulder ogres leer.

The road which wound down into the swamp, among rotting stumps and rank hummocks and scummy, snake-haunted pools and bogs, crawled past the hut. Many people passed that way these days, but few saw old Ezra, save a glimpse of a yellow face, peering through the fungus-screened windows, itself like an ugly fungus.

Old Ezra the miser partook much of the quality of the swamp, for he was gnarled and bent and sullen; his fingers were like clutching parasitic plants and his locks hung like drab moss above eyes trained to the murk of the swamplands. His eyes were like a dead man's, yet hinted of depths abysmal and loathsome as the dead lakes of the swamplands.

These eyes gleamed now at the man who stood in front of his hut. This man was tall and gaunt and dark, his face was haggard and claw-marked, and he was bandaged of arm and leg. Somewhat behind this man stood a number of villagers.

"You are Ezra of the swamp road?"

"Aye, and what want ye of me?"

"Where is your cousin Gideon, the maniac youth who abode with you?"

"Gideon?"

"Aye."

"He wandered away into the swamp and never came back. No doubt he lost his way and was set upon by wolves or died in a quagmire or was struck by an adder."

"How long ago?"

"Over a year."

"Aye. Hark ye, Ezra the miser. Soon after your cousin's disappearance, a countryman, coming home across the moors, was set upon by some unknown fiend and torn to pieces, and thereafter it became death to cross those moors. First men of the countryside, then strangers who wandered over the fen, fell to the clutches of the thing. Many men have died, since the first one.

"Last night I crossed the moors, and heard the flight and pursuing of another victim, a stranger who knew not the evil of the moors. Ezra the miser, it was a fearful thing, for the wretch twice broke from the fiend, terribly wounded, and each time the demon caught and dragged him down again. And at last he fell dead at my very feet, done to death in a manner that would freeze the statue of a saint."

The villagers moved restlessly and murmured fearfully to each other, and old Ezra's eyes shifted furtively. Yet the somber expression of Solomon Kane never altered, and his condor-like stare seemed to transfix the miser.

"Aye, aye!" muttered old Ezra hurriedly; "a bad thing, a bad thing! Yet why do you tell this thing to me?"

"Aye, a sad thing. Harken further, Ezra. The fiend came out of the shadows and I fought with it, over the body of its victim. Aye, how I overcame it, I know not, for the battle was hard and long, but the powers of good and light were on my side, which are mightier than the powers of Hell.

"At the last I was stronger, and it broke from me and fled, and I followed to no avail. Yet before it fled it whispered to me a monstrous truth."

Old Ezra started, stared wildly, seemed to shrink into himself.

"Nay, why tell me this?" he muttered.

"I returned to the village and told my tale," said Kane, "for I knew that now I had the power to rid the moors of its curse forever. Ezra, come with us!"

"Where?" gasped the miser.

"To the rotting oak on the moors."

Ezra reeled as though struck; he screamed incoherently and turned to flee.

On the instant, at Kane's sharp order, two brawny villagers sprang forward and seized the miser. They twisted the dagger from his withered hand, and pinioned his arms, shuddering as their fingers encountered his clammy flesh.

Kane motioned them to follow, and turning strode up the trail, followed by the villagers, who found their strength taxed to the utmost in their task of bearing their prisoner along. Through the swamp they went and out, taking a little-used trail which led up over the low hills and out on the moors.

The sun was sliding down the horizon and old Ezra stared at it with bulging eyes — stared as if he could not gaze enough. Far out on the moors reared up the great oak tree, like a gibbet, now only a decaying shell. There Solomon Kane halted.

Old Ezra writhed in his captor's grasp and made inarticulate noises.

"Over a year ago," said Solomon Kane, "you, fearing that your insane cousin Gideon would tell men of your cruelties to him, brought him away from the swamp by the very trail by which we came, and murdered him here in the night."

Ezra cringed and snarled.

"You can not prove this lie!"

Kane spoke a few words to an agile villager. The youth clambered up the rotting bole of the tree and from a crevice, high up, dragged something that fell with a clatter at the feet of the miser. Ezra went limp with a terrible shriek.

The object was a man's skeleton, the skull cleft.

"You — how knew you this? You are Satan!" gibbered old Ezra.

Kane folded his arms.

"The thing I fought last night told me this thing as we reeled in battle, and I followed it to this tree. *For the fiend is Gideon's ghost.*"

Ezra shrieked again and fought savagely.

"You knew," said Kane somberly, "you knew what thing did these deeds. You feared the ghost of the maniac, and that is why you chose to leave his body on the fen instead of concealing it in the swamp. For you knew the ghost would haunt the place of his death. He was insane in life, and in death he did not know where to find his slayer; else he had come to you in your hut. He hates no man but you, but his mazed spirit can not tell one man from another, and he slays all, lest he let his killer escape. Yet he will know you and rest in peace forever after. Hate hath made of his ghost a solid thing that can rend and slay, and though he feared you terribly in life, in death he fears you not."

Kane halted. He glanced at the sun.

"All this I had from Gideon's ghost, in his yammerings and his whisperings and his shrieking silences. Naught but your death will lay that ghost."

Ezra listened in breathless silence and Kane pronounced the words of his doom.

"A hard thing it is," said Kane somberly, "to sentence a man to death in cold blood and in such a manner as I have in mind, but you must die that others may live — and God knoweth you deserve death.

"You shall not die by noose, bullet or sword, but at the talons of him you slew — for naught else will satiate him."

At these words Ezra's brain shattered, his knees gave way and he fell groveling and screaming for death, begging them to burn him at the stake, to flay him alive. Kane's face was set like death, and the villagers, the fear rousing their cruelty, bound the screeching wretch to the oak tree, and one of them bade him make his peace with God. But Ezra made no answer, shrieking in a high shrill voice with unbearable monotony. Then the villager would have struck the miser across the face, but Kane stayed him.

"Let him make his peace with Satan, whom he is more like to meet," said the Puritan grimly. "The sun is about to set. Loose his cords so that he may work loose by dark, since it is better to meet death free and unshackled than bound like a sacrifice."

As they turned to leave him, old Ezra yammered and gibbered unhuman sounds and then fell silent, staring at the sun with terrible intensity.

They walked away across the fen, and Kane flung a last look at the grotesque form bound to the tree, seeming in the uncertain light like a great fungus growing to the bole. And suddenly the miser screamed hideously:

"Death! Death! There are skulls in the stars!"

"Life was good to him, though he was gnarled and churlish and evil," Kane sighed. "Mayhap God has a place for such souls where fire and sacrifice may cleanse them of their dross as fire cleans the forest of fungous things. Yet my heart is heavy within me."

"Nay, sir," one of the villagers spoke, "you have done but the will of God, and good alone shall come of this night's deed."

"Nay," answered Kane heavily, "I know not — I know not."

The sun had gone down and night spread with amazing swiftness, as if great shadows came rushing down from unknown voids to cloak the world with hurrying darkness. Through the thick night came a weird echo, and the men halted and looked back the way they had come.

Nothing could be seen. The moor was an ocean of shadows and the tall grass about them bent in long waves before the faint wind, breaking the deathly stillness with breathless murmurings.

Then far away the red disk of the moon rose over the fen, and for an instant a grim silhouette was etched blackly against it. A shape came flying across the face of the moon — a bent, grotesque thing whose feet seemed scarcely to touch the earth; and close behind came a thing like a flying shadow — a nameless, shapeless horror.

A moment the racing twain stood out boldly against the moon; then they merged into one unnamable, formless mass, and vanished in the shadows.

Far across the fen sounded a single shriek of terrible laughter.

CRETE

Weird Tales, February 1929

The green waves wash above us
Who slumber in the bay
As washed the tide of ages
That swept our race away.

Our cities — dusty ruins;
Our galleys — deep-sea slime;
Our very ghosts, forgotten,
Bow to the sweep of Time.

Our land lies stark before it
As we to alien spears,
But, ah, the love we bore it
Outlasts the crawling years.

Ah, jeweled spires at even —
The lute's soft golden sigh —
The Lion-Gates of Knossos
When dawn was in the sky.

MOON MOCKERY

Weird Tales, April 1929

I walked in Tara's Wood one summer night,
  And saw, amid the still, star-haunted skies,
  A slender moon in silver mist arise,
And hover on the hill as if in fright.
Burning, I seized her veil and held her tight:
  An instant all her glow was in my eyes;
  Then she was gone, swift as a white bird flies,
And I went down the hill in opal light.

And soon I was aware, as down I came,
  That all was strange and new on every side;
    Strange people went about me to and fro,
And when I spoke with trembling mine own name
  They turned away, but one man said: "He died
    In Tara Wood, a hundred years ago."

RATTLE OF BONES

Weird Tales, June 1929

"Landlord, ho!" The shout broke the lowering silence and reverberated through the black forest with sinister echoing.

"This place hath a forbidding aspect, meseemeth."

Two men stood in front of the forest tavern. The building was low, long and rambling, built of heavy logs. Its small windows were heavily barred and the door was closed. Above the door its sinister sign showed faintly — a cleft skull.

This door swung slowly open and a bearded face peered out. The owner of the face stepped back and motioned his guests to enter — with a grudging gesture it seemed. A candle gleamed on a table; a flame smoldered in the fireplace.

"Your names?"

"Solomon Kane," said the taller man briefly.

"Gaston l'Armon," the other spoke curtly. "But what is that to you?"

"Strangers are few in the Black Forest," grunted the host, "bandits many. Sit at yonder table and I will bring food."

The two men sat down, with the bearing of men who have traveled far. One was a tall gaunt man, clad in a featherless hat and somber black garments, which set off the dark pallor of his forbidding face. The other was of a different type entirely, bedecked with lace and plumes, although his finery was somewhat stained from travel. He was handsome in a bold way, and his restless eyes shifted from side to side, never still an instant.

The host brought wine and food to the rough-hewn table and then stood back in the shadows, like a somber image. His features, now receding into vagueness, now luridly etched in the firelight as it leaped and flickered, were masked in a beard which seemed almost animal-like in thickness. A great nose curved above this beard and two small red eyes stared unblinkingly at his guests.

"Who are you?" suddenly asked the younger man.

"I am the host of the Cleft Skull Tavern," sullenly replied the other. His tone seemed to challenge his questioner to ask further.

"Do you have many guests?" l'Armon pursued.

"Few come twice," the host grunted.

Kane started and glanced up straight into those small red eyes, as if he sought for some hidden meaning in the host's words. The flaming eyes seemed to dilate, then dropped sullenly before the Englishman's cold stare.

"I'm for bed," said Kane abruptly, bringing his meal to a close. "I must take up my journey by daylight."

"And I," added the Frenchman. "Host, show us to our chambers."

Black shadows wavered on the walls as the two followed their silent host down a long, dark hall. The stocky, broad body of their guide seemed to grow and expand in the light of the small candle which he carried, throwing a long, grim shadow behind him.

At a certain door he halted, indicating that they were to sleep there. They entered; the host lit a candle with the one he carried, then lurched back the way he had come.

In the chamber the two men glanced at each other. The only furnishings of the room were a couple of bunks, a chair or two and a heavy table.

"Let us see if there be any way to make fast the door," said Kane. "I like not the looks of mine host."

"There are racks on door and jamb for a bar," said Gaston, "but no bar."

"We might break up the table and use its pieces for a bar," mused Kane.

"*Mon Dieu*," said l'Armon, "you are timorous, *m'sieu*."

Kane scowled. "I like not being murdered in my sleep," he answered gruffly.

"My faith!" the Frenchman laughed. "We are chance met — until I overtook you on the forest road an hour before sunset, we had never seen each other."

"I have seen you somewhere before," answered Kane, "though I can not now recall where. As for the other, I assume every man is an honest fellow until he shows me he is a rogue; moreover, I am a light sleeper and slumber with a pistol at hand."

The Frenchman laughed again.

"I was wondering how *m'sieu* could bring himself to sleep in the room with a stranger! Ha! Ha! All right, *m'sieu* Englishman, let us go forth and take a bar from one of the other rooms."

Taking the candle with them, they went into the corridor. Utter silence reigned and the small candle twinkled redly and evilly in the thick darkness.

"Mine host hath neither guests nor servants," muttered Solomon Kane. "A strange tavern! What is the name, now? These German words come not easily to me — the Cleft Skull? A bloody name, i'faith."

They tried the rooms next to theirs, but no bar rewarded their search. At last they came to the last room at the end of the corridor. They entered. It was furnished like the rest, except that the door was provided with a small barred opening, and fastened from the outside with a heavy bolt, which was secured at one end to the door-jamb. They raised the bolt and looked in.

"There should be an outer window, but there is not," muttered Kane. "Look!"

The floor was stained darkly. The walls and the one bunk were hacked in places, great splinters having been torn away.

"Men have died in here," said Kane, somberly. "Is yonder not a bar fixed in the wall?"

"Aye, but 'tis made fast," said the Frenchman, tugging at it. "The —"

A section of the wall swung back and Gaston gave a quick exclamation. A small, secret room was revealed, and the two men bent over the grisly thing that lay upon its floor.

"The skeleton of a man!" said Gaston. "And behold, how his bony leg is shackled to the floor! He was imprisoned here and died."

"Nay," said Kane, "the skull is cleft — methinks mine host had a grim reason for the name of his hellish tavern. This man, like us, was no doubt a wanderer who fell into the fiend's hands."

"Likely," said Gaston without interest; he was engaged in idly working the great iron ring from the skeleton's leg bones. Failing in this, he drew his sword and with an exhibition of remarkable strength cut the chain which joined the ring on the leg to a ring set deep in the log floor.

"Why should he shackle a skeleton to the floor?" mused the Frenchman. "*Monbleu!* 'Tis a waste of good chain. Now, *m'sieu*," he ironically addressed the white heap of bones, "I have freed you and you may go where you like!"

"Have done!" Kane's voice was deep. "No good will come of mocking the dead."

"The dead should defend themselves," laughed l'Armon.

"Somehow, I will slay the man who kills me, though my corpse climb up forty fathoms of ocean to do it."

Kane turned toward the outer door, closing the door of the secret room behind him. He liked not this talk which smacked of demonry and witchcraft; and he was in haste to face the host with the charge of his guilt.

As he turned, with his back to the Frenchman, he felt the touch of cold steel against his neck and knew that a pistol muzzle was pressed close beneath the base of his brain.

"Move not, *m'sieu*!" The voice was low and silky. "Move not, or I will scatter your few brains over the room."

The Puritan, raging inwardly, stood with his hands in air while l'Armon slipped his pistols and sword from their sheaths.

"Now you can turn," said Gaston, stepping back.

Kane bent a grim eye on the dapper fellow, who stood bare-headed now, hat in one hand, the other hand leveling his long pistol.

"Gaston the Butcher!" said the Englishman somberly. "Fool that I was to trust a Frenchman! You range far, murderer! I remember you now, with that cursed great hat off — I saw you in Calais some years agone."

"Aye — and now you will see me never again. What was that?"

"Rats exploring yon skeleton," said Kane, watching the bandit like a hawk, waiting for a single slight wavering of that black gun muzzle. "The sound was of the rattle of bones."

"Like enough," returned the other. "Now, *M'sieu* Kane, I know you carry considerable money on your person. I had thought to wait until you slept and then slay you, but the opportunity presented itself and I took it. You trick easily."

"I had little thought that I should fear a man with whom I had broken bread," said Kane, a deep timbre of slow fury sounding in his voice.

The bandit laughed cynically. His eyes narrowed as he began to back slowly toward the outer door. Kane's sinews tensed involuntarily; he gathered himself like a giant wolf about to launch himself in a death leap, but Gaston's hand was like a rock and the pistol never trembled.

"We will have no death plunges after the shot," said Gaston. "Stand still, *m'sieu*; I have seen men killed by dying men, and I wish to have distance enough between us to preclude that possibility. My faith — I will shoot, you will roar and charge, but you will die before you reach me with your bare hands. And mine host will have another skeleton in his secret niche. That is, if I do not kill him myself. The fool knows me not nor I him, moreover —"

The Frenchman was in the doorway now, sighting along the barrel. The candle, which had been stuck in a niche on the wall, shed a weird and flickering light which did not extend past the doorway. And with the suddenness of death, from the darkness behind Gaston's back, a broad, vague form rose up and a gleaming blade swept down. The Frenchman went to his knees like a butchered ox, his brains spilling from his cleft skull. Above him towered the figure of the host, a wild and terrible spectacle, still holding the hanger with which he had slain the bandit.

"Ho! ho!" he roared. "Back!"

Kane had leaped forward as Gaston fell, but the host thrust into his very face a long pistol which he held in his left hand.

"Back!" he repeated in a tigerish roar, and Kane retreated from the menacing weapon and the insanity in the red eyes.

The Englishman stood silent, his flesh crawling as he sensed a deeper and more hideous threat than the Frenchman had offered. There was something inhuman about this man, who now swayed to and fro like some great forest beast while his mirthless laughter boomed out again.

"Gaston the Butcher!" he shouted, kicking the corpse at his feet. "Ho! ho! My fine brigand will hunt no more! I had heard of this fool who roamed the Black Forest — he wished gold and he found death! Now your gold shall be mine; and more than gold — vengeance!"

"I am no foe of yours," Kane spoke calmly.

"All men are my foes! Look — the marks on my wrists! See — the marks on my ankles! And deep in my back — the kiss of the knout! And deep in my brain, the wounds of the years of the cold, silent cells where I lay as punishment for a crime I never committed!" The voice broke in a hideous, grotesque sob.

Kane made no answer. This man was not the first he had seen whose brain had shattered amid the horrors of the terrible Continental prisons.

"But I escaped!" the scream rose triumphantly. "And here I

make war on all men ... What was that?"

Did Kane see a flash of fear in those hideous eyes?

"My sorcerer is rattling his bones!" whispered the host, then laughed wildly. "Dying, he swore his very bones would weave a net of death for me. I shackled his corpse to the floor, and now, deep in the night, I hear his bare skeleton clash and rattle as he seeks to be free, and I laugh, I laugh! Ho! ho! How he yearns to rise and stalk like old King Death along these dark corridors when I sleep, to slay me in my bed!"

Suddenly the insane eyes flared hideously: "You were in that secret room, you and this dead fool! Did he talk to you?"

Kane shuddered in spite of himself. Was it insanity or did he actually hear the faint rattle of bones, as if the skeleton had moved slightly? Kane shrugged his shoulders; rats will even tug at dusty bones.

The host was laughing again. He sidled around Kane, keeping the Englishman always covered, and with his free hand opened the door. All was darkness within, so that Kane could not even see the glimmer of the bones on the floor.

"All men are my foes!" mumbled the host, in the incoherent manner of the insane. "Why should I spare any man? Who lifted a hand to my aid when I lay for years in the vile dungeons of Karlsruhe — and for a deed never proven? Something happened to my brain, then. I became as a wolf — a brother to these of the Black Forest to which I fled when I escaped.

"They have feasted, my brothers, on all who lay in my tavern — all except this one who now clashes his bones, this magician from Russia. Lest he come stalking back through the black shadows when night is over the world, and slay me — for who may slay the dead? — I stripped his bones and shackled him. His sorcery was not powerful enough to save him from me, but all men know that a dead magician is more evil than a living one. Move not, Englishman! Your bones I shall leave in this secret room beside this one, to —"

The maniac was standing partly in the doorway of the secret room, now, his weapon still menacing Kane. Suddenly he seemed to topple backward, and vanished in the darkness; and at the same instant a vagrant gust of wind swept down the outer corridor and slammed the door shut behind him. The candle on the wall flickered and went out. Kane's groping hands, sweeping over the floor, found a pistol, and he straightened, facing the door where the maniac had vanished. He stood in the utter darkness, his blood freezing, while a hideous muffled screaming came from the secret room, intermingled with the dry, grisly rattle of fleshless bones. Then silence fell.

Kane found flint and steel and lighted the candle. Then, holding it in one hand and the pistol in the other, he opened the secret door.

"Great God!" he muttered as cold sweat formed on his body. "This thing is beyond all reason, yet with mine own eyes I see it! Two vows have here been kept, for Gaston the Butcher swore that even in death he would avenge his slaying, and his was the hand which set yon fleshless monster free. And he —"

The host of the Cleft Skull lay lifeless on the floor of the secret room, his bestial face set in lines of terrible fear; and deep in his broken neck were sunk the bare fingerbones of the sorcerer's skeleton.

FORBIDDEN MAGIC

Weird Tales, July 1929

There came to me a Shape one summer night
  When all the world lay silent in the stars
  And moonlight crossed my room with ghostly bars.
It whispered hints of weird unhallowed sight;
I followed, then in waves of spectral light
  Mounted the shimmery ladders of my soul,
  Where moon-pale spiders, huge as dragons, stole —
Great forms like moths with wings of whispy white.

Then round the world the sighing of the loon
  Shook misty lakes beneath the false dawn's gleams.
  Rose-tinted shone the skyline's minaret.
  I rose in fear and then with blood and sweat
  Beat out the iron fabrics of my dreams
And shaped of them a web to snare the moon.

THE SHADOW KINGDOM

Weird Tales, August 1929

1. A King Comes Riding

The blare of the trumpets grew louder, like a deep golden tide surge, like the soft booming of the evening tides against the silver beaches of Valusia. The throng shouted, women flung roses from the roofs as the rhythmic chiming of silver hoofs came clearer and the first of the mighty array swung into view in the broad white street that curved round the golden-spired Tower of Splendor.

First came the trumpeters, slim youths, clad in scarlet, riding with a flourish of long, slender golden trumpets; next the bowmen, tall men from the mountains; and behind these the heavily armed footmen, their broad shields clashing in unison, their long spears swaying in perfect rhythm to their stride. Behind them came the mightiest soldiery in all the world, the Red Slayers, horsemen, splendidly mounted, armed in red from helmet to spur. Proudly they sat their steeds, looking neither to right nor to left, but aware of the shouting for all that. Like bronze statues they were, and there was never a waver in the forest of spears that reared above them.

Behind those proud and terrible ranks came the motley files of the mercenaries, fierce, wild-looking warriors, men of Mu and of Kaa-u and of the hills of the east and the isles of the west. They bore spears and heavy swords, and a compact group that marched somewhat apart were the bowmen of Lemuria. Then came the light foot of the nation, and more trumpeters brought up the rear.

A brave sight, and a sight which aroused a fierce thrill in the soul of Kull, king of Valusia. Not on the Topaz Throne at the front of the regal Tower of Splendor sat Kull, but in the saddle, mounted on a great stallion, a true warrior king. His mighty arm swung up in reply to the salutes as the hosts passed. His fierce eyes passed the gorgeous trumpeters with a casual glance, rested longer on the following soldiery; they blazed with a ferocious light as the Red Slayers halted in front of him with a clang of arms and a rearing of steeds, and tendered him the crown salute. They narrowed slightly as the mercenaries strode by. They saluted no one, the mercenaries. They walked with shoulders flung back, eyeing Kull boldly and straightly, albeit with a certain appreciation; fierce eyes, unblinking; savage eyes, staring from beneath shaggy manes and heavy brows.

And Kull gave back a like stare. He granted much to brave men, and there were no braver in all the world, not even among the wild tribesmen who now disowned him. But Kull was too much the savage to have any great love for these. There were too many feuds. Many were age-old enemies of Kull's nation, and though the name of Kull was now a word accursed among the mountains and valleys of his people, and though Kull had put them from his mind, yet the old hates, the ancient passions still lingered. For Kull was no Valusian but an Atlantean.

The armies swung out of sight around the gem-blazing shoulders of the Tower of Splendor and Kull reined his stallion about and started toward the palace at an easy gait, discussing the review with the commanders that rode with him, using not many words, but saying much.

"The army is like a sword," said Kull, "and must not be allowed to rust." So down the street they rode, and Kull gave no heed to any of the whispers that reached his hearing from the throngs that still swarmed the streets.

"That is Kull, see! Valka! But what a king! And what a man! Look at his arms! His shoulders!"

And an undertone of more sinister whisperings: "Kull! Ha, accursed usurper from the pagan isles" — "Aye, shame to Valusia that a barbarian sits on the Throne of Kings." . . .

Little did Kull heed. Heavy-handed had he seized the decaying throne of ancient Valusia and with a heavier hand did he hold it, a man against a nation.

After the council chamber, the social palace where Kull replied to the formal and laudatory phrases of the lords and ladies, with carefully hidden, grim amusement at such frivolities; then the lords and ladies took their formal departure and Kull leaned back upon the ermine throne and contemplated matters of state until an attendant requested permission from the great king to speak, and announced an emissary from the Pictish embassy.

Kull brought his mind back from the dim mazes of Valusian statecraft where it had been wandering, and gazed upon the Pict with little favor. The man gave back the gaze of the king without flinching. He was a lean-hipped, massive-chested warrior of middle height, dark, like all his race, and strongly built. From strong, immobile features gazed dauntless and inscrutable eyes.

"The chief of the Councilors, Ka-nu of the tribe, right hand of the king of Pictdom, sends greetings and says: 'There is a throne at the feast of the rising moon for Kull, king of kings, lord of lords, emperor of Valusia.'"

"Good," answered Kull. "Say to Ka-nu the Ancient, ambassador of the western isles, that the king of Valusia will quaff wine with him when the moon floats over the hills of Zalgara."

Still the Pict lingered. "I have a word for the king, not" — with a contemptuous flip of his hand — "for these slaves."

Kull dismissed the attendants with a word, watching the Pict warily.

The man stepped nearer, and lowered his voice: "Come alone to feast tonight, lord king. Such was the word of my chief."

The king's eyes narrowed, gleaming like gray sword steel, coldly.

"Alone?"

"Aye."

They eyed each other silently, their mutual tribal enmity seething beneath their cloak of formality. Their mouths spoke the cultured speech, the conventional court phrases of a highly polished race, a race not their own, but from their eyes gleamed the primal traditions of the elemental savage. Kull might be the king of Valusia and the Pict might be an emissary to her courts, but there in the throne hall of kings, two tribesmen glowered at each other, fierce and wary, while ghosts of wild wars and world-ancient feuds whispered to each.

To the king was the advantage and he enjoyed it to its fullest extent. Jaw resting on hand, he eyed the Pict, who stood like an image of bronze, head flung back, eyes unflinching.

Across Kull's lips stole a smile that was more a sneer.

"And so I am to come — alone?" Civilization had taught him to speak by innuendo and the Pict's dark eyes glittered, though he made no reply. "How am I to know that you come from Ka-nu?"

"I have spoken," was the sullen response.

"And when did a Pict speak truth?" sneered Kull, fully aware that the Picts never lied, but using this means to enrage the man.

"I see your plan, king," the Pict answered imperturbably. "You wish to anger me. By Valka, you need go no further! I am angry enough. And I challenge you to meet me in single battle, spear, sword or dagger, mounted or afoot. Are you king or man?"

Kull's eyes glinted with the grudging admiration a warrior must needs give a bold foeman, but he did not fail to use the chance of further annoying his antagonist.

"A king does not accept the challenge of a nameless savage," he sneered, "nor does the emperor of Valusia break the Truce of Ambassadors. You have leave to go. Say to Ka-nu I will come alone."

The Pict's eyes flashed murderously. He fairly shook in the grasp of the primitive blood-lust; then, turning his back squarely upon the king of Valusia, he strode across the Hall of Society and vanished through the great door.

Again Kull leaned back upon the ermine throne and meditated.

So the chief of the Council of Picts wished him to come alone? But for what reason? Treachery? Grimly Kull touched the hilt of his great sword. But scarcely. The Picts valued too greatly the alliance with Valusia to break it for any feudal reason. Kull might be a warrior of Atlantis and hereditary enemy of all Picts, but too, he was king of Valusia, the most potent ally of the Men of the West.

Kull reflected long upon the strange state of affairs that made him ally of ancient foes and foe of ancient friends. He rose and paced restlessly across the hall, with the quick, noiseless tread of a lion. Chains of friendship, tribe and tradition had he broken to satisfy his ambition. And, by Valka, god of the sea and the land, he had realized that ambition! He was king of Valusia — a fading, degenerate Valusia, a Valusia living mostly in dreams of bygone glory, but still a mighty land and the greatest of the Seven Empires. Valusia — Land of Dreams, the tribesmen named it, and sometimes it seemed to Kull that he moved in a dream. Strange to him were the intrigues of court and palace, army and people. All was like a masquerade, where men and women hid their real thoughts with a smooth mask. Yet the seizing of the throne had been easy — a bold snatching of opportunity, the swift whirl of swords, the slaying of a tyrant of whom men had wearied unto death, short, crafty plotting with ambitious statesmen out of favor at court — and Kull, wandering adventurer, Atlantean exile, had swept up to the dizzy heights of his dreams: he was lord of Valusia, king of kings. Yet now it seemed that the seizing was far easier than the keeping. The sight of the Pict had brought back youthful associations to his mind, the free, wild savagery of his boyhood. And now a strange feeling of dim unrest, of unreality, stole over him as of late it had been doing. Who was he, a straightforward man of the seas and the mountain, to rule a race strangely and terribly wise with the mysticisms of antiquity? An ancient race —

"I am Kull!" said he, flinging back his head as a lion flings back his mane. "I am Kull!"

His falcon gaze swept the ancient hall. His self-confidence flowed back. . . . And in a dim nook of the hall a tapestry moved — slightly.

2. Thus Spake the Silent Halls of Valusia

The moon had not risen, and the garden was lighted with torches aglow in silver cressets when Kull sat down in the throne before the table of Ka-nu, ambassador of the western isles. At his right hand sat the ancient Pict, as much unlike an emissary of that fierce race as a man could be. Ancient was Ka-nu and wise in state-craft, grown old in the game. There was no elemental hatred in the eyes that looked at Kull appraisingly; no tribal traditions hindered his judgments. Long associations with the statesmen of the civilized nations had swept away such cobwebs. Not "Who and what is this man?" was the question ever foremost in Ka-nu's mind, but "Can I use this man, and how?" Tribal prejudices he used only to further his own schemes.

And Kull watched Ka-nu, answering his conversation briefly, wondering if civilization would make of him a thing like the Pict. For Ka-nu was soft and paunchy. Many years had stridden across the sky-rim since Ka-nu had wielded a sword. True, he was old, but Kull had seen men older than he in the forefront of battle. The Picts were a long-lived race. A beautiful girl stood at Ka-nu's elbow, refilling his goblet, and she was kept busy. Meanwhile Ka-nu kept up a running fire of jests and comments, and Kull, secretly contemptuous of his garrulity, nevertheless missed none of his shrewd humor.

At the banquet were Pictish chiefs and statesmen, the latter jovial and easy in their manner, the warriors formally courteous, but plainly hampered by their tribal affinities. Yet Kull, with a tinge of envy, was cognizant of the freedom and ease of the affair as contrasted with like affairs of the Valusian court. Such freedom prevailed in the rude camps of Atlantis — Kull shrugged his shoulders. After all, doubtless Ka-nu, who had seemed to have forgotten he was a Pict as far as time-hoary custom and prejudice went, was right and he, Kull, would better become a Valusian in mind as in name.

At last when the moon had reached her zenith, Ka-nu, having eaten and drunk as much as any three men there, leaned back upon his divan with a comfortable sigh and said, "Now, get you gone, friends, for the king and I would converse on such matters as concerns not children. Yes, you too, my pretty; yet first let me kiss those ruby lips — so; now dance away, my rose-bloom."

Ka-nu's eyes twinkled above his white beard as he surveyed Kull, who sat erect, grim and uncompromising.

"You are thinking, Kull," said the old statesman, suddenly, "that Ka-nu is a useless old reprobate, fit for nothing except to guzzle wine and kiss wenches!"

In fact, this remark was so much in line with his actual thoughts, and so plainly put, that Kull was rather startled, though he gave no sign.

Ka-nu gurgled and his paunch shook with his mirth. "Wine is red and women are soft," he remarked tolerantly. "But — ha-ha! — think not old Ka-nu allows either to interfere with business."

Again he laughed, and Kull moved restlessly. This seemed much like being made sport of, and the king's scintillant eyes began to glow with a feline light.

Ka-nu reached for the wine-pitcher, filled his beaker and glanced questioningly at Kull, who shook his head irritably.

"Aye," said Ka-nu equably, "it takes an old head to stand strong drink. I am growing old, Kull, so why should you young men begrudge me such pleasures as we oldsters must find? Ah me, I grow ancient and withered, friendless and cheerless."

But his looks and expressions failed far of bearing out his words. His rubicund countenance fairly glowed, and his eyes sparkled, so that his white beard seemed incongruous. Indeed, he looked remarkably elfin, reflected Kull, who felt vaguely resentful. The old scoundrel had lost all of the primitive virtues of his race and of Kull's race, yet he seemed more pleased in his aged days than otherwise.

"Hark ye, Kull," said Ka-nu, raising an admonitory finger, "'tis a chancy thing to laud a young man, yet I must speak my true thoughts to gain your confidence."

"If you think to gain it by flattery —"

"Tush. Who spake of flattery? I flatter only to disguard."

There was a keen sparkle in Ka-nu's eyes, a cold glimmer that did not match his lazy smile. He knew men, and he knew that to gain his end he must smite straight with this tigerish barbarian, who, like a wolf scenting a snare, would scent out unerringly any falseness in the skein of his word-web.

"You have power, Kull," said he, choosing his words with more care than he did in the council rooms of the nation, "to make yourself mightiest of all kings, and restore some of the lost glories of Valusia. So. I care little for Valusia — though the women and wine be excellent—save for the fact that the stronger Valusia is, the stronger is the Pict nation. More, with an Atlantean on the throne, eventually Atlantis will become united —"

Kull laughed in harsh mockery. Ka-nu had touched an old wound.

"Atlantis made my name accursed when I went to seek fame and fortune among the cities of the world. We — they — are age-old foes of the Seven Empires, greater foes of the allies of the Empires, as you should know."

Ka-nu tugged his beard and smiled enigmatically.

"Nay, nay. Let it pass. But I know whereof I speak. And then warfare will cease, wherein there is no gain; I see a world of peace and prosperity — man loving his fellow man — the good supreme. All this can you accomplish — *if you live!*"

"Ha!" Kull's lean hand closed on his hilt and he half-rose, with a sudden movement of such dynamic speed that Ka-nu, who fancied men as some men fancy blooded horses, felt his old blood leap with a sudden thrill. Valka, what a warrior! Nerves and sinews of steel and fire, bound together with the perfect coordination, the fighting instinct, that makes the terrible warrior.

But none of Ka-nu's enthusiasm showed in his mildly sarcastic tone.

"Tush. Be seated. Look about you. The gardens are deserted, the seats empty, save for ourselves. You fear not *me?*"

Kull sank back, gazing about him warily.

"There speaks the savage," mused Ka-nu. "Think you if I planned treachery I would enact it here where suspicion would be sure to fall upon me? Tut. You young tribesmen have much to learn. There were my chiefs who were not at ease because you were born among the hills of Atlantis, and you despise me in your secret mind because I am a Pict. Tush. I see you as Kull, king of Valusia, not as Kull, the reckless Atlantean, leader of the raiders who harried the western isles. So you should see in me, not a Pict but an international man, a figure of the world. Now to that figure, hark! If you were slain tomorrow who would be king?"

"Kaanuub, baron of Blaal."

"Even so. I object to Kaanuub for many reasons, yet most of all for the fact that he is but a figurehead."

"How so? He was my greatest opponent, but I did not know that he championed any cause but his own."

"The night can hear," answered Ka-nu obliquely. "There are worlds within worlds. But you may trust me and you may trust Brule, the Spear-slayer. Look!" He drew from his robes a bracelet of gold representing a winged dragon coiled thrice, with three horns of ruby on the head.

"Examine it closely. Brule will wear it on his arm when he comes to you tomorrow night so that you may know him. Trust Brule as you trust yourself, and do what he tells you to. And in proof of trust, look ye!"

And with the speed of a striking hawk, the ancient snatched something from his robes, something that flung a weird green light over them, and which he replaced in an instant.

"The stolen gem!" exclaimed Kull recoiling. "The green jewel from the Temple of the Serpent! Valka! You! And why do you show it to me?"

"To save your life. To prove my trust. If I betray your trust, deal with me likewise. You hold my life in your hand. Now I could not be false to you if I would, for a word from you would be my doom."

Yet for all his words the old scoundrel beamed merrily and seemed vastly pleased with himself.

"But why do you give me this hold over you?" asked Kull, becoming more bewildered each second.

"As I told you. Now, you see that I do not intend to deal you false, and tomorrow night when Brule comes to you, you will follow his advice without fear of treachery. Enough. An escort waits outside to ride to the palace with you, lord."

Kull rose. "But you have told me nothing."

"Tush. How impatient are youths!" Ka-nu looked more like a

mischievous elf than ever. "Go you and dream of thrones and power and kingdoms, while I dream of wine and soft women and roses. And fortune ride with you, King Kull."

As he left the garden, Kull glanced back to see Ka-nu still reclining lazily in his seat, a merry ancient, beaming on all the world with jovial fellowship.

A mounted warrior waited for the king just without the garden and Kull was slightly surprized to see that it was the same that had brought Ka-nu's invitation. No word was spoken as Kull swung into the saddle nor as they clattered along the empty streets.

The color and the gayety of the day had given away to the eerie stillness of night. The city's antiquity was more than ever apparent beneath the bent, silver moon. The huge pillars of the mansions and palaces towered up into the stars. The broad stairways, silent and deserted, seemed to climb endlessly until they vanished in the shadowy darkness of the upper realms. Stairs to the stars, thought Kull, his imaginative mind inspired by the weird grandeur of the scene.

Clang! Clang! Clang! sounded the silver hoofs on the broad, moon-flooded streets, but otherwise there was no sound. The age of the city, its incredible antiquity, was almost oppressive to the king; it was as if the great silent buildings laughed at him, noiselessly, with unguessable mockery. And what secrets did they hold?

"You are young," said the palaces and the temples and the shrines, "but we are old. The world was wild with youth when we were reared. You and your tribe shall pass, but we are invincible, indestructible. We towered above a strange world, ere Atlantis and Lemuria rose from the sea; we still shall reign when the green waters sigh for many a restless fathom above the spires of Lemuria and the hills of Atlantis and when the isles of the Western Men are the mountains of a strange land.

"How many kings have we watched ride down these streets before Kull of Atlantis was even a dream in the mind of Ka, bird of Creation? Ride on, Kull of Atlantis; greater shall follow you; greater came before you. They are dust; they are forgotten; we stand; we know; we are. Ride, ride on, Kull of Atlantis; Kull the king, Kull the fool!"

And it seemed to Kull that the clashing hoofs took up the silent refrain to beat it into the night with hollow re-echoing mockery:

"Kull — the — king! Kull — the — fool!"

Glow, moon; you light a king's way! Gleam, stars; you are torches in the train of an emperor! And clang, silver-shod hoofs; you herald that Kull rides through Valusia.

Ho! Awake, Valusia! It is Kull that rides, Kull the king!

"We have known many kings," said the silent halls of Valusia.

And so in a brooding mood Kull came to the palace, where his bodyguard, men of the Red Slayers, came to take the rein of the great stallion and escort Kull to his rest. There the Pict, still sullenly speechless, wheeled his steed with a savage wrench of the rein and fled away in the dark like a phantom; Kull's heightened imagination pictured him speeding through the silent streets like a goblin out of the Elder World.

There was no sleep for Kull that night, for it was nearly dawn and he spent the rest of the night hours pacing the throne room, and pondering over what had passed. Ka-nu had told him nothing, yet he had put himself in Kull's complete power. At what had he hinted when he had said the baron of Blaal was naught but a figurehead? And who was this Brule who was to come to him by night, wearing the mystic armlet of the dragon? And why? Above all, why had Ka-nu shown him the green gem of terror, stolen long ago from the temple of the Serpent, for which the world would rock in wars were it known to the weird and terrible keepers of that temple, and from whose vengeance not even Ka-nu's ferocious tribesmen might be able to save him? But Ka-nu knew he was safe, reflected Kull, for the statesman was too shrewd to expose himself to risk without profit. But was it to throw the king off his guard and pave the way to treachery? Would Ka-nu dare let him live now? Kull shrugged his shoulders.

3. They That Walk the Night

The moon had not risen when Kull, hand to hilt, stepped to a window. The windows opened upon the great inner gardens of the royal palace, and the breezes of the night, bearing the scents of spice trees, blew the filmy curtains about. The king looked out. The walks and groves were deserted; carefully trimmed trees were bulky shadows; fountains nearby flung their slender sheen of silver in the starlight and distant fountains rippled steadily. No guards walked those gardens, for so closely were the outer walls guarded that it seemed impossible for any invader to gain access to them.

Vines curled up the walls of the palace, and even as Kull mused upon the ease with which they might be climbed, a segment of shadow detached itself from the darkness below the window and a bare, brown arm curved up over the sill. Kull's great sword hissed halfway from the sheath; then the king halted. Upon the muscular forearm gleamed the dragon armlet shown him by Ka-nu the night before.

The possessor of the arm pulled himself up over the sill and into the room with the swift, easy motion of a climbing leopard.

"You are Brule?" asked Kull, and then stopped in surprize not unmingled with annoyance and suspicion; for the man was he whom Kull had taunted in the hall of Society; the same who had escorted him from the Pictish embassy.

"I am Brule, the Spear-slayer," answered the Pict in a guarded voice; then swiftly, gazing closely in Kull's face, he said, barely above a whisper:

"Ka nama kaa lajerama!"

Kull started. "Ha! What mean you?"

"Know you not?"

"Nay, the words are unfamiliar; they are of no language I ever heard — and yet, by Valka! — somewhere — I have heard —"

"Aye," was the Pict's only comment. His eyes swept the room, the study room of the palace. Except for a few tables, a divan or two and great shelves of books of parchment, the room was barren compared to the grandeur of the rest of the palace.

"Tell me, king, who guards the door?"

"Eighteen of the Red Slayers. But how come you, stealing through the gardens by night and scaling the walls of the palace?"

Brule sneered. "The guards of Valusia are blind buffaloes. I could steal their girls from under their noses. I stole amid them and they saw me not nor heard me. And the walls — I could scale them without the aid of vines. I have hunted tigers on the foggy beaches when the sharp east breezes blew the mist in from seaward and I have climbed the steeps of the western sea mountain. But come — nay, touch this armlet."

He held out his arm and, as Kull complied wonderingly, gave an apparent sigh of relief.

"So. Now throw off those kingly robes; for there are ahead of you this night such deeds as no Atlantean ever dreamed of."

Brule himself was clad only in a scanty loin-cloth through which was thrust a short, curved sword.

"And who are you to give me orders?" asked Kull, slightly resentful.

"Did not Ka-nu bid you follow me in all things?" asked the Pict irritably, his eyes flashing momentarily. "I have no love for you, lord, but for the moment I have put the thought of feuds from my mind. Do you likewise. But come."

Walking noiselessly, he led the way across the room to the door. A slide in the door allowed a view of the outer corridor, unseen from without, and the Pict bade Kull look.

"What see you?"

"Naught but the eighteen guardsmen."

The Pict nodded, motioned Kull to follow him across the room. At a panel in the opposite wall Brule stopped and fumbled there a moment. Then with a light movement he stepped back, drawing his sword as he did so. Kull gave an exclamation as the panel swung silently open, revealing a dimly lighted passageway.

"A secret passage!" swore Kull softly. "And I knew nothing of it! By Valka, someone shall dance for this!"

"Silence!" hissed the Pict.

Brule was standing like a bronze statue as if straining every nerve for the slightest sound; something about his attitude made Kull's hair prickle slightly, not from fear but from some eerie anticipation. Then beckoning, Brule stepped through the secret doorway which stood open behind them. The passage was bare, but not dust covered as should have been the case with an unused secret corridor. A vague, gray light filtered through somewhere, but the source of it was not apparent. Every few feet Kull saw doors, invisible, as he knew, from the outside, but easily apparent from within.

"The palace is a very honeycomb," he muttered.

"Aye. Night and day you are watched, king, by many eyes."

The king was impressed by Brule's manner. The Pict went forward slowly, warily, half-crouching, blade held low and thrust forward. When he spoke it was in a whisper and he continually flung glances from side to side.

The corridor turned sharply and Brule warily gazed past the turn.

"Look!" he whispered. "But remember! No word! No sound — on your life!"

Kull cautiously gazed past him. The corridor changed just at the bend to a flight of steps. And then Kull recoiled. At the foot of those stairs lay the eighteen Red Slayers who were that night stationed to watch the king's study room. Brule's grip upon his mighty arm and Brule's fierce whisper at his shoulder alone kept Kull from leaping down those stairs.

"Silent, Kull! Silent, in Valka's name!" hissed the Pict. "These corridors are empty now, but I risked much in showing you, that you might then believe what I had to say. Back now to the room of study." And he retraced his steps, Kull following; his mind in a turmoil of bewilderment.

"This is treachery," muttered the king, his steel-gray eyes a-smolder, "foul and swift! Mere minutes have passed since those men stood at guard."

Again in the room of study Brule carefully closed the secret panel and motioned Kull to look again through the slit of the outer door. Kull gasped audibly. *For without stood the eighteen guardsmen!*

"This is sorcery!" he whispered, half-drawing his sword. "Do dead men guard the king?"

"Aye!" came Brule's scarcely audible reply; there was a strange expression in the Pict's scintillant eyes. They looked squarely into each other's eyes for an instant, Kull's brow wrinkled in a puzzled scowl as he strove to read the Pict's inscrutable face. Then Brule's lips, barely moving, formed the words:

"The — snake — that — speaks!"

"Silent!" whispered Kull, laying his hand over Brule's mouth. "That is death to speak! That is a name accursed!"

The Pict's fearless eyes regarded him steadily.

"Look again, King Kull. Perchance the guard was changed."

"Nay, those are the same men. In Valka's name, this is sorcery — this is insanity! I saw with my own eyes the bodies of those men, not eight minutes agone. Yet there they stand."

Brule stepped back, away from the door, Kull mechanically following.

"Kull, what know ye of the traditions of this race ye rule?"

"Much — and yet, little. Valusia is so old —"

"Aye," Brule's eyes lighted strangely, "we are but barbarians — infants compared to the Seven Empires. Not even they themselves know how old they are. Neither the memory of man nor the annals of the historians reach back far enough to tell us when the first men came up from the sea and built cities on the shore. But Kull, *men were not always ruled by men!*"

The king started. Their eyes met.

"Aye, there is a legend of my people —"

"And mine!" broke in Brule. "That was before we of the isles were allied with Valusia. Aye, in the reign of Lion-fang, seventh war chief of the Picts, so many years ago no man remembers how many. Across the sea we came, from the isles of the sunset, skirting the shores of Atlantis, and falling upon the beaches of Valusia with fire and sword. Aye, the long white beaches resounded with the clash of spears, and the night was like day from the flame of the burning castles. And the king, the king of Valusia, who died on the red sea sands that dim day —" His voice trailed off; the two stared at each other, neither speaking; then each nodded.

"Ancient is Valusia!" whispered Kull. "The hills of Atlantis and Mu were isles of the sea when Valusia was young."

The night breeze whispered through the open window. Not the free, crisp sea air such as Brule and Kull knew and reveled in, in their land, but a breath like a whisper from the past, laden with musk, scents of forgotten things, breathing secrets that were hoary when the world was young.

The tapestries rustled, and suddenly Kull felt like a naked child before the inscrutable wisdom of the mystic past. Again the sense of unreality swept upon him. At the back of his soul stole dim, gigantic phantoms, whispering monstrous things. He sensed that Brule experienced similar thoughts. The Pict's eyes were fixed upon his face with a fierce intensity. Their glances met. Kull felt warmly a sense of comradeship with this member of an enemy tribe. Like rival leopards turning at bay against hunters, these two savages made common cause against the inhuman powers of antiquity.

Brule again led the way back to the secret door. Silently they entered and silently they proceeded down the dim corridor, taking the opposite direction from that in which they had previously traversed it. After a while the Pict stopped and pressed close to one of the secret doors, bidding Kull look with him through the hidden slot.

"This opens upon a little-used stair which leads to a corridor running past the study-room door."

They gazed, and presently, mounting the stair silently, came a silent shape.

"Tu! Chief councilor!" exclaimed Kull. "By night and with bared dagger! How, what means this, Brule?"

"Murder! And foulest treachery!" hissed Brule. "Nay" — as Kull would have flung the door aside and leaped forth — "we are lost if you meet him here, for more lurk at the foot of those stairs. Come!"

Half-running, they darted back along the passage. Back through the secret door Brule led, shutting it carefully behind them, then across the chamber to an opening into a room seldom used. There he swept aside some tapestries in a dim corner nook and, drawing Kull with him, stepped behind them. Minutes dragged. Kull could hear the breeze in the other room blowing the window curtains about, and it seemed to him like the murmur of ghosts. Then through the door, stealthily, came Tu, chief councilor of the king. Evidently he had come through the study room and, finding it empty, sought his victim where he was most likely to be.

He came with upraised dagger, walking silently. A moment he halted, gazing about the apparently empty room, which was lighted dimly by a single candle. Then he advanced cautiously, apparently at a loss to understand the absence of the king. He stood before the hiding place — and —

"Slay!" hissed the Pict.

Kull with a single mighty leap hurled himself into the room. Tu spun, but the blinding, tigerish speed of the attack gave him no chance for defense or counter-attack. Sword steel flashed in the dim light and grated on bone as Tu toppled backward, Kull's sword standing out between his shoulders.

Kull leaned above him, teeth bared in the killer's snarl, heavy brows a-scowl above eyes that were like the gray ice of the cold sea. Then he released the hilt and recoiled, shaken, dizzy, the hand of death at his spine.

For as he watched, Tu's face became strangely dim and unreal; the features mingled and merged in a seemingly impossible manner. Then, like a fading mask of fog, the face suddenly vanished and in its stead gaped and leered *a monstrous serpent's head!*

"Valka!" gasped Kull, sweat beading his forehead, and again: "Valka!"

Brule leaned forward, face immobile. Yet his glittering eyes mirrored something of Kull's horror.

"Regain your sword, lord king," said he. "There are yet deeds to be done."

Hesitantly Kull set his hand to the hilt. His flesh crawled as he set his foot upon the terror which lay at their feet, and as some jerk of muscular reaction caused the frightful mouth to gape suddenly, he recoiled, weak with nausea. Then, wrathful at himself, he plucked forth his sword and gazed more closely at the nameless thing that had been known as Tu, chief councilor. Save for the reptilian head, the thing was the exact counterpart of a man.

"A man with the head of a snake!" Kull murmured. "This, then, is a priest of the serpent god?"

"Aye. Tu sleeps unknowing. These fiends can take any form they will. That is, they can, by a magic charm or the like, fling a web of sorcery about their faces, as an actor dons a mask, so that they resemble anyone they wish to."

"Then the old legends were true," mused the king; "the grim old tales few dare even whisper, lest they die as blasphemers, are no fantasies. By Valka, I had thought — I had guessed — but it seems beyond the bounds of reality. Ha! The guardsmen outside the door —"

"They too are snake-men. Hold! What would you do?"

"Slay them!" said Kull between his teeth.

"Strike at the skull if at all," said Brule. "Eighteen wait without the door and perhaps a score more in the corridors. Hark ye, king, Ka-nu learned of this plot. His spies have pierced the inmost fastnesses of the snake priests and they brought hints of a plot. Long ago he discovered the secret passageways of the palace, and at his command I studied the map thereof and came here by night to aid you, lest you die as other kings of Valusia have died. I came alone for the reason that to send more would have roused suspicion. Many could not steal into the palace as I did. Some of the foul conspiracy you have seen. Snake-men guard your door, and that one, as Tu, could pass anywhere else in the palace; in the morning, if the priests failed, the real guards would be holding their places again, nothing knowing, nothing remembering; there to take the blame if the priests succeeded. But stay you here while I dispose of this carrion."

So saying, the Pict shouldered the frightful thing stolidly and vanished with it through another secret panel. Kull stood alone, his mind a-whirl. Neophytes of the mighty serpent, how many lurked among his cities? How might he tell the false from the true? Aye, how many of his trusted councilors, his generals, were men? He could be certain — of whom?

The secret panel swung inward and Brule entered.

"You were swift."

"Aye!" The warrior stepped forward, eyeing the floor. "There is gore upon the rug. See?"

Kull bent forward; from the corner of his eye he saw a blur of movement, a glint of steel. Like a loosened bow he whipped erect, thrusting upward. The warrior sagged upon the sword, his own clattering to the floor. Even at that instant Kull reflected grimly that it was appropriate that the traitor should meet his death upon the sliding, upward thrust used so much by his race. Then, as Brule slid from the sword to sprawl motionless on the floor, the face began to merge and fade, and as Kull caught his breath, his hair a-prickle, the human features vanished and there the jaws of a great snake gaped hideously, the terrible beady eyes venomous even in death.

"He was a snake priest all the time!" gasped the king. "Valka! What an elaborate plan to throw me off my guard! Ka-nu there, is he a man? Was it Ka-nu to whom I talked in the gardens? Almighty Valka!" as his flesh crawled with a horrid thought; "are the people of Valusia men or are they *all* serpents?"

Undecided he stood, idly seeing that the thing named Brule no longer wore the dragon armlet. A sound made him wheel.

Brule was coming through the secret door.

"Hold!" upon the arm upthrown to halt the king's hovering sword gleamed the dragon armlet. "Valka!" The Pict stopped short. Then a grim smile curled his lips.

"By the gods of the seas! These demons are crafty past reckoning. For it must be that that one lurked in the corridors, and seeing me go carrying the carcass of that other, took my appearance. So. I have another to do away with."

"Hold!" there was the menace of death in Kull's voice; "I have seen two men turn to serpents before my eyes. How may I know if you are a true man?"

Brule laughed. "For two reasons, King Kull. No snake-man wears this" — he indicated the dragon armlet — "nor can any say these words," and again Kull heard the strange phrase: *"Ka nama kaa lajerama."*

"Ka nama kaa lajerama," Kull repeated mechanically. "Now where, in Valka's name, have I heard that? I have not! And yet — and yet —"

"Aye, you remember, Kull," said Brule. "Through the dim corridors of memory those words lurk; though you never heard them in this life, yet in the bygone ages they were so terribly impressed upon the soul mind that never dies, that they will always strike dim chords in your memory, though you be reincarnated for a million years to come. For that phrase has come secretly down the grim and bloody eons, since when, uncounted centuries ago, those words were watchwords for the race of men who battled with the grisly beings of the Elder Universe. For none but a real man of men may speak them, whose jaws and mouth are shaped different from any other creature. Their meaning has been forgotten but not the words themselves."

"True," said Kull. "I remember the legends — Valka!" He stopped short, staring, for suddenly, like the silent swinging wide of a mystic door, misty, unfathomed reaches opened in the recesses of his consciousness and for an instant he seemed to gaze back through the vastnesses that spanned life and life; seeing through the vague and ghostly fogs dim shapes reliving dead centuries — men in combat with hideous monsters, vanquishing a planet of frightful terrors. Against a gray, ever-shifting background moved strange nightmare forms, fantasies of lunacy and fear; and man, the jest of the gods, the blind, wisdomless striver from dust to dust, following the long bloody trail of his destiny, knowing not why, bestial, blundering, like a great murderous child, yet feeling somewhere a spark of divine fire. . . . Kull drew a hand across his brow, shaken; these sudden glimpses into the abysses of memory always startled him.

"They are gone," said Brule, as if scanning his secret mind; "the bird-women, the harpies, the bat-men, the flying fiends, the wolf-people, the demons, the goblins — all save such as this being that lies at our feet, and a few of the wolf-men. Long and terrible was the war, lasting through the bloody centuries, since first the first men, risen from the mire of apedom, turned upon those who then ruled the world. And at last mankind conquered, so long ago that naught but dim legends come to us through the ages. The snake-people were the last to go, yet at last men conquered even them and drove them forth into the waste lands of the world, there to mate with true snakes until some day, say the sages, the horrid breed shall vanish utterly. Yet the Things returned in crafty guise as men grew soft and degenerate, forgetting ancient wars. Ah, that was a grim and secret war! Among the men of the Younger Earth stole the frightful monsters of the Elder Planet, safeguarded by their horrid wisdom and mysticisms, taking all forms and shapes, doing deeds of horror secretly. No man knew who was true man and who false. No man could trust any man. Yet by means of their own craft they formed ways by which the false might be known from the true. Men took for a sign and a standard the figure of the flying dragon, the winged dinosaur, a monster of past ages, which was the greatest foe of the serpent. And men used those words which I spoke to you as a sign and symbol, for as I said, none but a true man can repeat them. So mankind triumphed. Yet again the fiends came after the years of forgetfulness had gone by — for man is still an ape in that he forgets what is not ever before his eyes. As priests they came; and for that men in their luxury and might had by then lost faith in the old religions and worships, the snake-men, in the guise of teachers of a new and truer cult, built a monstrous religion about the worship of the serpent god. Such is their power that it is now death to repeat the old legends of the snake-people, and people bow again to the serpent god in new form; and blind fools that they are, the great hosts of men see no connection between this power and the power men overthrew eons ago. As priests the snake-men are content to rule — and yet —" He stopped.

"Go on." Kull felt an unaccountable stirring of the short hair at the base of his scalp.

"Kings have reigned as true men in Valusia," the Pict whispered, "and yet, slain in battle, have died serpents — as died he who fell beneath the spear of Lion-fang on the red beaches when we of the isles harried the Seven Empires. And how can this be, Lord Kull? These kings were born of women and lived as men! This — the true kings died in secret — as you would have died tonight — and priests of the Serpent reigned in their stead, no man knowing."

Kull cursed between his teeth. "Aye, it must be. No one has ever seen a priest of the Serpent and lived, that is known. They live in utmost secrecy."

"The statecraft of the Seven Empires is a mazy, monstrous thing," said Brule. "There the true men know that among them glide the spies of the serpent, and the men who are the Serpent's allies — such as Kaanuub, baron of Blaal — yet no man dares seek to unmask a suspect lest vengeance befall him. No man trusts his fellow and the true statesmen dare not speak to each other what is in the minds of all. Could they be sure, could a snake-man or plot be unmasked before them all, then would the power of the Serpent be more than half-broken; for all would then ally and make common cause, sifting out the traitors. Ka-nu alone is of sufficient shrewdness and courage to cope with them, and even Ka-nu learned only enough of their plot to tell me what would happen — what has happened up to this time. Thus far I was prepared; from now on we must trust to our luck and our craft. Here and now I think we are safe; those snake-men without the door dare not leave their post lest true men come here unexpectedly. But tomorrow they will try something else, you may be sure. Just what they will do, none can say, not even Ka-nu; but we must stay at each other's sides, King Kull, until we conquer or both be dead. Now come with me while I take this carcass to the hiding-place where I took the other being."

Kull followed the Pict with his grisly burden through the secret panel and down the dim corridor. Their feet, trained to the silence of the wilderness, made no noise. Like phantoms they glided through the ghostly light, Kull wondering that the corridors should be deserted; at every turn he expected to run full upon some frightful apparition. Suspicion surged back upon him; was this Pict leading him into ambush? He fell back a pace or two behind Brule, his ready sword hovering at the Pict's unheeding back. Brule should die first if he meant treachery. But if the Pict was aware of the king's suspicion, he showed no sign. Stolidly he tramped along, until they came to a room, dusty and long unused, where moldy tapestries hung heavy. Brule drew aside some of these and concealed the corpse behind them.

Then they turned to retrace their steps, when suddenly Brule halted with such abruptness that he was closer to death than he knew; for Kull's nerves were on edge.

"Something moving in the corridor," hissed the Pict. "Ka-nu said these ways would be empty, yet —"

He drew his sword and stole into the corridor, Kull following warily.

A short way down the corridor a strange, vague glow appeared that came toward them. Nerves a-leap, they waited, backs to the corridor wall; for what they knew not, but Kull heard Brule's breath hiss through his teeth and was reassured as to Brule's loyalty.

The glow merged into a shadowy form. A shape vaguely like a man it was, but misty and illusive, like a wisp of fog, that grew more tangible as it approached, but never fully material. A face looked at them, a pair of luminous great eyes, that seemed to hold all the tortures of a million centuries. There was no menace in that face, with its dim, worn features, but only a great pity — and that face — that face —

"Almighty gods!" breathed Kull, an icy hand at his soul; "Eallal, king of Valusia, who died a thousand years ago!"

Brule shrank back as far as he could, his narrow eyes widened in a blaze of pure horror, the sword shaking in his grip, unnerved for the first time that weird night. Erect and defiant stood Kull, instinctively holding his useless sword at the ready; flesh a-crawl, hair a-prickle, yet still a king of kings, as ready to challenge the powers of the unknown dead as the powers of the living.

The phantom came straight on, giving them no heed; Kull shrank back as it passed them, feeling an icy breath like a breeze from the arctic snow. Straight on went the shape with slow, silent footsteps, as if the chains of all the ages were upon those vague feet; vanishing about a bend of the corridor.

"Valka!" muttered the Pict, wiping the cold beads from his brow; "That was no man! That was a ghost!"

"Aye!" Kull shook his head wonderingly. "Did you not recognize the face? That was Eallal, who reigned in Valusia a thousand years ago and who was found hideously murdered in his throne room — the room now known as the Accursed Room. Have you not seen his statue in the Fame Room of Kings?"

"Yes, I remember the tale now. Gods, Kull! That is another sign of the frightful and foul power of the snake priests — that king was slain by snake-people and thus his soul became their slave, to do their bidding throughout eternity! For the sages have ever maintained that if a man is slain by a snake-man his ghost becomes their slave."

A shudder shook Kull's gigantic frame. "Valka! But what a fate! Hark ye" — his fingers closed upon Brule's sinewy arm like steel — "hark ye! If I am wounded unto death by these foul monsters, swear that ye will smite your sword through my breast lest my soul be enslaved."

"I swear," answered Brule, his fierce eyes lighting. "And do ye the same by me, Kull."

Their strong right hands met in a silent sealing of their bloody bargain.

4. Masks

Kull sat upon his throne and gazed broodingly out upon the sea of faces turned toward him. A courtier was speaking in evenly modulated tones, but the king scarcely heard him. Close by, Tu, chief councilor, stood ready at Kull's command, and each time the king looked at him, Kull shuddered inwardly. The surface of court life was as the unrippled surface of the sea between tide and tide. To the musing king the affairs of the night before seemed as a dream, until his eyes dropped to the arm of his throne. A brown, sinewy hand rested there, upon the wrist of which gleamed a dragon armlet; Brule stood beside his throne and ever the Pict's fierce secret whisper brought him back from the realm of unreality in which he moved.

No, that was no dream, that monstrous interlude. As he sat upon his throne in the Hall of Society and gazed upon the courtiers, the ladies, the lords, the statesmen, he seemed to see their faces as things of illusion, things unreal, existent only as shadows and mockeries of substance. Always he had seen their faces as masks, but before he had looked on them with contemptuous tolerance, thinking to see beneath the masks shallow, puny souls, avaricious, lustful, deceitful; now there was a grim undertone, a sinister meaning, a vague horror that lurked beneath the smooth masks. While he exchanged courtesies with some nobleman or councilor he seemed to see the smiling face fade like smoke and the frightful jaws of a serpent gaping there. How many of those he looked upon were horrid, inhuman monsters, plotting his death, beneath the smooth mesmeric illusion of a human face?

Valusia — land of dreams and nightmares — a kingdom of the shadows, ruled by phantoms who glided back and forth behind the painted curtains, mocking the futile king who sat upon the throne — himself a shadow.

And like a comrade shadow Brule stood by his side, dark eyes glittering from immobile face. A real man, Brule! And Kull felt his friendship for the savage become a thing of reality and sensed that

Brule felt a friendship for him beyond the mere necessity of state-craft.

And what, mused Kull, were the realities of life? Ambition, power, pride? The friendship of man, the love of women — which Kull had never known — battle, plunder, what? Was it the real Kull who sat upon the throne or was it the real Kull who had scaled the hills of Atlantis, harried the far isles of the sunset, and laughed upon the green roaring tides of the Atlantean sea? How could a man be so many different men in a lifetime? For Kull knew that there were many Kulls and he wondered which was the real Kull. After all, the priests of the Serpent merely went a step further in their magic, for all men wore masks, and many a different mask with each different man or woman; and Kull wondered if a serpent did not lurk under every mask.

So he sat and brooded in strange, mazy thought-ways, and the courtiers came and went and the minor affairs of the day were completed, until at last the king and Brule sat alone in the Hall of Society save for the drowsy attendants.

Kull felt a weariness. Neither he nor Brule had slept the night before, nor had Kull slept the night before that, when in the gardens of Ka-nu he had had his first hint of the weird things to be. Last night nothing further had occurred after they had returned to the study room from the secret corridors, but they had neither dared nor cared to sleep. Kull, with the incredible vitality of a wolf, had aforetime gone for days upon days without sleep, in his wild savage days, but now his mind was edged from constant thinking and from the nerve-breaking eeriness of the past night. He needed sleep, but sleep was furthest from his mind.

And he would not have dared sleep if he had thought of it. Another thing that had shaken him was the fact that though he and Brule had kept a close watch to see if, or when, the study-room guard was changed, yet it was changed without their knowledge; for the next morning those who stood on guard were able to repeat the magic words of Brule, but they remembered nothing out of the ordinary. They thought that they had stood at guard all night, as usual, and Kull said nothing to the contrary. He believed them true men, but Brule had advised absolute secrecy, and Kull also thought it best.

Now Brule leaned over the throne, lowering his voice so not even a lazy attendant could hear: "They will strike soon, I think,

Kull. A while ago Ka-nu gave me a secret sign. The priests know that we know of their plot, of course, but they know not how much we know. We must be ready for any sort of action. Ka-nu and the Pictish chiefs will remain within hailing distance now until this is settled one way or another. Ha, Kull, if it comes to a pitched battle, the streets and the castles of Valusia will run red!"

Kull smiled grimly. He would greet any sort of action with a ferocious joy. This wandering in a labyrinth of illusion and magic was extremely irksome to his nature. He longed for the leap and clang of swords, for the joyous freedom of battle.

Then into the Hall of Society came Tu again, and the rest of the councilors.

"Lord king, the hour of the council is at hand and we stand ready to escort you to the council room."

Kull rose, and the councilors bent the knee as he passed through the way opened by them for his passage, rising behind him and following. Eyebrows were raised as the Pict strode defiantly behind the king, but no one dissented. Brule's challenging gaze swept the smooth faces of the councilors with the defiance of an intruding savage.

The group passed through the halls and came at last to the council chamber. The door was closed, as usual, and the councilors arranged themselves in the order of their rank before the dais upon which stood the king. Like a bronze statue Brule took up his stand behind Kull.

Kull swept the room with a swift stare. Surely no chance of treachery here. Seventeen councilors there were, all known to him; all of them had espoused his cause when he ascended the throne.

"Men of Valusia —" he began in the conventional manner, then halted, perplexed. The councilors had risen as a man and were moving toward him. There was no hostility in their looks, but their actions were strange for a council room. The foremost was close to him when Brule sprang forward, crouched like a leopard.

"*Ka nama kaa lajerama!*" his voice crackled through the sinister silence of the room and the foremost councilor recoiled, hand flashing to his robes; and like a spring released Brule moved and the man pitched headlong to the glint of his sword — headlong he pitched and lay still while his face faded and became the head of a mighty snake.

"Slay, Kull!" rasped the Pict's voice. "They be all serpent men!"

The rest was a scarlet maze. Kull saw the familiar faces dim like fading fog and in their places gaped horrid reptilian visages as the whole band rushed forward. His mind was dazed but his giant body faltered not.

The singing of his sword filled the room, and the onrushing flood broke in a red wave. But they surged forward again, seemingly willing to fling their lives away in order to drag down the king. Hideous jaws gaped at him; terrible eyes blazed into his unblinkingly; a frightful fetid scent pervaded the atmosphere — the serpent scent that Kull had known in southern jungles. Swords and daggers leaped at him and he was dimly aware that they wounded him. But Kull was in his element; never before had he faced such grim foes but it mattered little; they lived, their veins held blood that could be spilt and they died when his great sword cleft their skulls or drove through their bodies. Slash, thrust, thrust and swing. Yet had Kull died there but for the man who crouched at his side, parrying and thrusting. For the king was clear berserk, fighting in the terrible Atlantean way, that seeks death to deal death; he made no effort to avoid thrusts and slashes, standing straight up and ever plunging forward, no thought in his frenzied mind but to slay. Not often did Kull forget his fighting craft in his primitive fury, but now some chain had broken in his soul, flooding his mind with a red wave of slaughter-lust. He slew a foe at each blow, but they surged about him, and time and again Brule turned a thrust that would have slain, as he crouched beside Kull, parrying and warding with cold skill, slaying not as Kull slew with long slashes and plunges, but with short overhand blows and upward thrusts.

Kull laughed, a laugh of insanity. The frightful faces swirled about him in a scarlet blaze. He felt steel sink into his arm and dropped his sword in a flashing arc that cleft his foe to the breast-bone. Then the mists faded and the king saw that he and Brule stood alone above a sprawl of hideous crimson figures who lay still upon the floor.

"Valka! What a killing!" said Brule, shaking the blood from his eyes. "Kull, had these been warriors who knew how to use the steel, we had died here. These serpent priests know naught of swordcraft and die easier than any men I ever slew. Yet had there been a few more, I think the matter had ended otherwise."

Kull nodded. The wild berserker blaze had passed, leaving a

mazed feeling of great weariness. Blood seeped from wounds on breast, shoulder, arm and leg. Brule, himself bleeding from a score of flesh wounds, glanced at him in some concern.

"Lord Kull, let us hasten to have your wounds dressed by the women."

Kull thrust him aside with a drunken sweep of his mighty arm.

"Nay, we'll see this through ere we cease. Go you, though, and have your wounds seen to — I command it."

The Pict laughed grimly. "Your wounds are more than mine, lord king —" he began, then stopped as a sudden thought struck him. "By Valka, Kull, this is not the council room!"

Kull looked about and suddenly other fogs seemed to fade. "Nay, this is the room where Eallal died a thousand years ago — since unused and named 'Accursed'."

"Then by the gods, they tricked us after all!" exclaimed Brule in a fury, kicking the corpses at their feet. "They caused us to walk like fools into their ambush! By their magic they changed the appearance of all —"

"Then there is further deviltry afoot," said Kull, "for if there be true men in the councils of Valusia they should be in the real council room now. Come swiftly."

And leaving the room with its ghastly keepers they hastened through halls that seemed deserted until they came to the real council room. Then Kull halted with a ghastly shudder. *From the council room sounded a voice speaking, and the voice was his!*

With a hand that shook he parted the tapestries and gazed into the room. There sat the councilors, counterparts of the men he and Brule had just slain, and upon the dais stood Kull, king of Valusia.

He stepped back, his mind reeling.

"This is insanity!" he whispered. "Am I Kull? Do I stand here or is that Kull yonder in very truth and am I but a shadow, a figment of thought?"

Brule's hand clutching his shoulder, shaking him fiercely, brought him to his senses.

"Valka's name, be not a fool! Can you yet be astounded after all we have seen? See you not that those are true men bewitched by a snake-man who has taken your form, as those others took their forms? By now you should have been slain and yon monster reigning in your stead, unknown by those who bowed to you. Leap and slay swiftly or else we are undone. The Red Slayers, true men, stand close on each hand and none but you can reach and slay him. Be swift!"

Kull shook off the onrushing dizziness, flung back his head in the old, defiant gesture. He took a long, deep breath as does a strong swimmer before diving into the sea; then, sweeping back the tapestries, made the dais in a single lion-like bound. Brule had spoken truly. There stood men of the Red Slayers, guardsmen trained to move quick as the striking leopard; any but Kull had died ere he could reach the usurper. But the sight of Kull, identical with the man upon the dais, held them in their tracks, their minds stunned for an instant, and that was long enough. He upon the dais snatched for his sword, but even as his fingers closed upon the hilt, Kull's sword stood out behind his shoulders and the thing that men had thought the king pitched forward from the dais to lie silent upon the floor.

"Hold!" Kull's lifted hand and kingly voice stopped the rush that had started, and while they stood astounded he pointed to the thing which lay before them — whose face was fading into that of a snake. They recoiled, and from one door came Brule and from another came Ka-nu.

These grasped the king's bloody hand and Ka-nu spoke: "Men of Valusia, you have seen with your own eyes. This is the true Kull, the mightiest king to whom Valusia has ever bowed. The power of the Serpent is broken and ye be all true men. King Kull, have you commands?"

"Lift that carrion," said Kull, and men of the guard took up the thing.

"Now follow me," said the king, and he made his way to the Accursed Room. Brule, with a look of concern, offered the support of his arm but Kull shook him off.

The distance seemed endless to the bleeding king, but at last he stood at the door and laughed fiercely and grimly when he heard the horrified ejaculations of the councilors.

At his orders the guardsmen flung the corpse they carried beside the others, and motioning all from the room Kull stepped out last and closed the door.

A wave of dizziness left him shaken. The faces turned to him, pallid and wonderingly, swirled and mingled in a ghostly fog. He felt the blood from his wound trickling down his limbs and he knew that what he was to do, he must do quickly or not at all.

His sword rasped from its sheath.

"Brule, are you there?"

"Aye!" Brule's face looked at him through the mist, close to his shoulder, but Brule's voice sounded leagues and eons away.

"Remember our vow, Brule. And now, bid them stand back."

His left arm cleared a space as he flung up his sword. Then with all his waning power he drove it through the door into the jamb, driving the great sword to the hilt and sealing the room forever.

Legs braced wide, he swayed drunkenly, facing the horrified councilors. "Let this room be doubly accursed. And let those rotting skeletons lie there forever as a sign of the dying might of the serpent. Here I swear that I shall hunt the serpent-men from land to land, from sea to sea, giving no rest until all be slain, that good triumph and the power of Hell be broken. This thing I swear — I — Kull — king — of — Valusia."

His knees buckled as the faces swayed and swirled. The councilors leaped forward, but ere they could reach him, Kull slumped to the floor, and lay still, face upward.

The councilors surged about the fallen king, chattering and shrieking. Ka-nu beat them back with his clenched fists, cursing savagely.

"Back, you fools! Would you stifle the little life that is yet in him? How, Brule, is he dead or will he live?" — to the warrior who bent above the prostrate Kull.

"Dead?" sneered Brule irritably. "Such a man as this is not so easily killed. Lack of sleep and loss of blood have weakened him — by Valka, he has a score of deep wounds, but none of them mortal. Yet have those gibbering fools bring the court women here at once."

Brule's eyes lighted with a fierce, proud light.

"Valka, Ka-nu, but here is such a man as I knew not existed in these degenerate days. He will be in the saddle in a few scant days and then may the serpent-men of the world beware of Kull of Valusia. Valka! But that will be a rare hunt! Ah, I see long years of prosperity for the world with such a king upon the throne of Valusia."

THE MIRRORS OF TUZUN THUNE

Weird Tales, September 1929

"A wild, weird clime that lieth sublime
Out of Space, out of Time."
— Poe.

There comes, even to kings, the time of great weariness. Then the gold of the throne is brass, the silk of the palace becomes drab. The gems in the diadem and upon the fingers of the women sparkle drearily like the ice of the white seas; the speech of men is as the empty rattle of a jester's bell and the feel comes of things unreal; even the sun is copper in the sky and the breath of the green ocean is no longer fresh.

Kull sat upon the throne of Valusia and the hour of weariness was upon him. They moved before him in an endless, meaningless panorama, men, women, priests, events and shadows of events; things seen and things to be attained. But like shadows they came and went, leaving no trace upon his consciousness, save that of a great mental fatigue. Yet Kull was not tired. There was a longing in him for things beyond himself and beyond the Valusian court. An unrest stirred in him and strange, luminous dreams roamed his soul. At his bidding there came to him Brule the Spear-slayer, warrior of Pictland, from the islands beyond the West.

"Lord king, you are tired of the life of the court. Come with me upon my galley and let us roam the tides for a space."

"Nay." Kull rested his chin moodily upon his mighty hand. "I am weary beyond all these things. The cities hold no lure for me — and the borders are quiet. I hear no more the sea-songs I heard when I lay as a boy on the booming crags of Atlantis, and the night was alive with blazing stars. No more do the green woodlands beckon me as of old. There is a strangeness upon me and a longing beyond life's longings. Go!"

Brule went forth in a doubtful mood, leaving the king brooding upon his throne. Then to Kull stole a girl of the court and whispered:

"Great king, seek Tuzun Thune, the wizard. The secrets of life and death are his, and the stars in the sky and the lands beneath the seas."

Kull looked at the girl. Fine gold was her hair and her violet eyes were slanted strangely; she was beautiful, but her beauty meant little to Kull.

"Tuzun Thune," he repeated. "Who is he?"

"A wizard of the Elder Race. He lives here, in Valusia, by the Lake of Visions in the House of a Thousand Mirrors. All things are known to him, lord king; he speaks with the dead and holds converse with the demons of the Lost Lands."

Kull arose.

"I will seek out this mummer; but no word of my going, do you hear?"

"I am your slave, my lord." And she sank to her knees meekly, but the smile of her scarlet mouth was cunning behind Kull's back and the gleam of her narrow eyes was crafty.

Kull came to the house of Tuzun Thune, beside the Lake of Visions. Wide and blue stretched the waters of the lake and many a fine palace rose upon its banks; many swan-winged pleasure boats drifted lazily upon its hazy surface and evermore there came the sound of soft music.

Tall and spacious, but unpretentious, rose the House of a Thousand Mirrors. The great doors stood open and Kull ascended the broad stair and entered, unannounced. There in a great chamber, whose walls were of mirrors, he came upon Tuzun Thune, the wizard. The man was ancient as the hills of Zalgara; like wrinkled leather was his skin, but his cold gray eyes were like sparks of sword steel.

"Kull of Valusia, my house is yours," said he, bowing with old-time courtliness and motioning Kull to a throne-like chair.

"You are a wizard, I have heard," said Kull bluntly, resting his chin upon his hand and fixing his somber eyes upon the man's face. "Can you do wonders?"

The wizard stretched forth his hand; his fingers opened and closed like a bird's claws.

"Is that not a wonder — that this blind flesh obeys the thoughts of my mind? I walk, I breathe, I speak — are they all not wonders?"

Kull meditated awhile, then spoke. "Can you summon up demons?"

"Aye. I can summon up a demon more savage than any in ghostland — by smiting you in the face."

Kull started, then nodded. "But the dead, can you talk to the dead?"

"I talk with the dead always — as I am talking now. Death begins with birth and each man begins to die when he is born; even now you are dead, King Kull, because you were born."

"But you, you are older than men become; do wizards never die?"

"Men die when their time comes. No later, no sooner. Mine has not come."

Kull turned these answers over in his mind.

"Then it would seem that the greatest wizard of Valusia is no more than an ordinary man, and I have been duped in coming here."

Tuzun Thune shook his head. "Men are but men, and the greatest men are they who soonest learn the simpler things. Nay, look into my mirrors, Kull."

The ceiling was a great many mirrors, and the walls were mirrors, perfectly jointed, yet many mirrors of many sizes and shapes.

"Mirrors are the world, Kull," droned the wizard. "Gaze into my mirrors and be wise."

Kull chose one at random and looked into it intently. The mirrors upon the opposite wall were reflected there, reflecting others, so that he seemed to be gazing down a long, luminous corridor, formed by mirror behind mirror; and far down this corridor moved a tiny figure. Kull looked long ere he saw that the figure was the reflection of himself. He gazed and a queer feeling of pettiness came over him; it seemed that that tiny figure was the true Kull, representing the real proportions of himself. So he moved away and stood before another.

"Look closely, Kull. That is the mirror of the past," he heard the wizard say.

Gray fogs obscured the vision, great billows of mist, ever heaving and changing like the ghost of a great river; through these fogs Kull caught swift fleeting visions of horror and strangeness; beasts and men moved there and shapes neither men nor beasts; great exotic blossoms glowed through the grayness; tall tropic trees towered high over reeking swamps, where reptilian monsters wallowed and bellowed; the sky was ghastly with flying dragons and the restless seas rocked and roared and beat endlessly along the muddy beaches. Man was not, yet man was the dream of the gods and strange were the nightmare forms that glided through the noisome jungles. Battle and onslaught were there, and frightful love. Death was there, for Life and Death go hand in hand. Across the slimy beaches of the world sounded the bellowing of the monsters, and incredible shapes loomed through the steaming curtain of the incessant rain.

"This is of the future."

Kull looked in silence.

"See you — what?"

"A strange world," said Kull heavily. "The Seven Empires are crumbled to dust and are forgotten. The restless green waves roar for many a fathom above the eternal hills of Atlantis; the mountains of Lemuria of the West are the islands of an unknown sea. Strange savages roam the elder lands and new lands flung strangely from the deeps, defiling the elder shrines. Valusia is vanished and all the nations of today; they of tomorrow are strangers. They know us not."

"Time strides onward," said Tuzun Thune calmly. "We live today; what care we for tomorrow — or yesterday? The Wheel turns and nations rise and fall; the world changes, and times return to savagery to rise again through the long ages. Ere Atlantis was, Valusia was, and ere Valusia was, the Elder Nations were. Aye, we, too, trampled the shoulders of lost tribes in our advance. You, who have come from the green sea hills of Atlantis to seize the ancient crown of Valusia, you think my tribe is old, we who held these lands ere the Valusians came out of the East, in the days before there were men in the sea lands. But men were here when the Elder Tribes rode out of the waste lands, and men before men, tribe before tribe. The nations pass and are forgotten, for that is the destiny of man."

"Yes," said Kull. "Yet is it not a pity that the beauty and glory of men should fade like smoke on a summer sea?"

"For what reason, since that is their destiny? I brood not over the lost glories of my race, nor do I labor for races to come. Live now, Kull, live now. The dead are dead; the unborn are not. What matters men's forgetfulness of you when you have forgotten yourself in the silent worlds of death? Gaze in my mirrors and be wise."

Kull chose another mirror and gazed into it.

"That is the mirror of the deepest magic; what see ye, Kull?"

"Naught but myself."

"Look closely, Kull; is it in truth you?"

Kull stared into the great mirror, and the image that was his reflection returned his gaze.

"I come before this mirror," mused Kull, chin on fist, "and I bring this man to life. This is beyond my understanding, since first I saw him in the still waters of the lakes of Atlantis, till I saw him again in the gold-rimmed mirrors of Valusia. He is I, a shadow of myself, part of myself — I can bring him into being or slay him at my will; yet" — he halted, strange thoughts whispering through the vast dim recesses of his mind like shadowy bats flying through a great cavern — "yet where is he when I stand not in front of a mirror? May it be in man's power thus lightly to form and destroy a shadow of life and existence? How do I know that when I step back from the mirror he vanishes into the void of Naught?

"Nay, by Valka, am I the man or is he? Which of us is the ghost of the other? Mayhap these mirrors are but windows through which we look into another world. Does he think the same of me? Am I no more than a shadow, a reflection of himself — to him, as he to me? And if I am the ghost, what sort of a world lives upon the other side of this mirror? What armies ride there and what kings rule? This world is all I know. Knowing naught of any other, how can I judge? Surely there are green hills there and booming seas and wide plains where men ride to battle. Tell me, wizard who are wiser than most men, tell me, are there worlds beyond our worlds?"

"A man has eyes, let him see," answered the wizard. "Who would see must first believe."

The hours drifted by and Kull still sat before the mirrors of Tuzun Thune, gazing into that which depicted himself. Sometimes it seemed that he gazed upon hard shallowness; at other times gigantic depths seemed to loom before him. Like the surface of the sea was the mirror of Tuzun Thune; hard as the sea in the sun's slanting beams, in the darkness of the stars, when no eye can pierce her deeps; vast and mystic as the sea when the sun smites her in such way that the watcher's breath is caught at the glimpse of tremendous abysses. So was the mirror in which Kull gazed.

At last the king rose with a sigh and took his departure still wondering. And Kull came again to the House of a Thousand Mirrors; day after day he came and sat for hours before the mirror. The eyes looked out at him, identical with his, yet Kull seemed to sense a difference — a reality that was not of him. Hour upon hour he would stare with strange intensity into the mirror; hour after hour the image gave back his gaze.

The business of the palace and of the council went neglected. The people murmured; Kull's stallion stamped restlessly in his stable and Kull's warriors diced and argued aimlessly with one another. Kull heeded not. At times he seemed on the point of discovering some vast, unthinkable secret. He no longer thought of the image in the mirror as a shadow of himself; the thing, to him, was an entity, similar in outer appearance, yet basically as far from Kull himself as the poles are far apart. The image, it seemed to Kull, had an individuality apart from Kull's; he was no more dependent on Kull than Kull was dependent on him. And day by day Kull doubted in which world he really lived; was he the shadow, summoned at will by the other? Did he instead of the other live in a world of delusion, the shadow of the real world?

Kull began to wish that he might enter the personality beyond the mirror for a space, to see what might be seen; yet should he manage to go beyond that door could he ever return? Would he find a world identical with the one in which he moved? A world, of which his was but a ghostly reflection? Which was reality and which illusion?

At times Kull halted to wonder how such thoughts and dreams had come to enter his mind and at times he wondered if they came of his own volition or — here his thoughts would become mazed. His meditations were his own; no man ruled his thoughts and he would summon them at his pleasure; yet could he? Were they not as bats, coming and going, not at his pleasure but at the bidding or ruling of — of whom? The gods? The Women who wove the webs of Fate? Kull could come to no conclusion, for at each mental step he became more and more bewildered in a hazy gray fog of illusory assertions and refutations. This much he knew: that strange visions entered his mind, like bats flying unbidden from the whispering void of non-existence; never had he thought these thoughts, but now they ruled his mind, sleeping and waking, so that he seemed to walk in a daze at times; and his sleep was fraught with strange, monstrous dreams.

"Tell me, wizard," he said, sitting before the mirror, eyes fixed intently upon his image, "how can I pass yon door? For of a truth, I am not sure that that is the real world and this the shadow; at least, that which I see must exist in some form."

"See and believe," droned the wizard. "Man must believe to accomplish. Form is shadow, substance is illusion, materiality is dream; man is because he believes he is; what is man but a dream of the gods? Yet man can be that which he wishes to be; form and substance, they are but shadows. The mind, the ego, the essence of the god-dream — that is real, that is immortal. See and believe, if you would accomplish, Kull."

The king did not fully understand; he never fully understood the enigmatical utterances of the wizard, yet they struck somewhere in his being a dim responsive chord. So day after day he sat before the mirrors of Tuzun Thune. Ever the wizard lurked behind him like a shadow.

Then came a day when Kull seemed to catch glimpses of strange lands; there flitted across his consciousness dim thoughts and recognitions. Day by day he had seemed to lose touch with the world; all things had seemed each succeeding day more ghostly and unreal; only the man in the mirror seemed like reality. Now Kull seemed to be close to the doors of some mightier worlds; giant vistas gleamed fleetingly; the fogs of unreality thinned, "form is shadow, substance is illusion; they are but shadows" sounded as if from some far country of his consciousness. He remembered the wizard's words and it seemed to him that now he almost understood — form and substance, could not he change himself at will, if he knew the master key that opened this door? What worlds within what worlds awaited the bold explorer?

The man in the mirror seemed smiling at him — closer, closer — a fog enwrapped all and the reflection dimmed suddenly — Kull knew a sensation of fading, of change, of merging —

"Kull!" the yell split the silence into a million vibratory fragments!

Mountains crashed and worlds tottered as Kull, hurled back by that frantic shout, made a superhuman effort, how or why he did not know.

A crash, and Kull stood in the room of Tuzun Thune before a shattered mirror, mazed and half-blind with bewilderment. There before him lay the body of Tuzun Thune, whose time had come at last, and above him stood Brule the Spear-slayer, sword dripping red and eyes wide with a kind of horror.

"Valka!" swore the warrior. "Kull, it was time I came!"

"Aye, yet what happened?" The king groped for words.

"Ask this traitress," answered the Spear-slayer, indicating a girl who crouched in terror before the king; Kull saw that it was she who first sent him to Tuzun Thune. "As I came in I saw you fading into yon mirror as smoke fades into the sky, by Valka! Had I not seen I would not have believed — you had almost vanished when my shout brought you back."

"Aye," muttered Kull, "I had almost gone beyond the door that time."

"This fiend wrought most craftily," said Brule. "Kull, do you not now see how he spun and flung over you a web of magic? Kaanuub of Blaal plotted with this wizard to do away with you, and this wench, a girl of Elder Race, put the thought in your mind so that you would come here. Kananu of the council learned of the plot today; I know not what you saw in that mirror, but with it Tuzun Thune enthralled your soul and almost by his witchery he changed your body to mist —"

"Aye." Kull was still mazed. "But being a wizard, having knowledge of all the ages and despising gold, glory and position, what could Kaanuub offer Tuzun Thune that would make of him a foul traitor?"

"Gold, power and position," grunted Brule. "The sooner you learn that men are men whether wizard, king or thrall, the better you will rule, Kull. Now what of her?"

"Naught, Brule," as the girl whimpered and groveled at Kull's feet. "She was but a tool. Rise, child, and go your ways; none shall harm you."

Alone with Brule, Kull looked for the last time on the mirrors of Tuzun Thune.

"Mayhap he plotted and conjured, Brule; nay, I doubt you not, yet — was it his witchery that was changing me to thin mist, or had I stumbled on a secret? Had you not brought me back, had I faded in dissolution or had I found worlds beyond this?"

Brule stole a glance at the mirrors, and twitched his shoulders as if he shuddered. "Aye. Tuzun Thune stored the wisdom of all the hells here. Let us begone, Kull, ere they bewitch me, too."

"Let us go, then," answered Kull, and side by side they went forth from the House of a Thousand Mirrors — where, mayhap, are prisoned the souls of men.

None look now in the mirrors of Tuzun Thune. The pleasure boats shun the shore where stands the wizard's house and no one goes in the house or to the room where Tuzun Thune's dried and withered carcass lies before the mirrors of illusion. The place is shunned as a place accursed, and though it stands for a thousand years to come, no footsteps shall echo there. Yet Kull upon his throne meditates often upon the strange wisdom and untold secrets hidden there and wonders. . . .

For there are worlds beyond worlds, as Kull knows, and whether the wizard bewitched him by words or by mesmerism, vistas did open to the king's gaze beyond that strange door, and Kull is less sure of reality since he gazed into the mirrors of Tuzun Thune.

THE MOOR GHOST

Weird Tales, September 1929

They haled him to the crossroads
  As day was at its close;
They hung him to the gallows
  And left him for the crows.

His hands in life were bloody,
  His ghost will not be still;
He haunts the naked moorlands
  About the gibbet hill.

And oft a lonely traveler
  Is found upon the fen
Whose dead eyes hold a horror
  Beyond the world of men.

The villagers then whisper,
  With accents grim and dour:
"This man has met at midnight
  The phantom of the moor."

RED THUNDER

JAPM: The Poetry Weekly, September 16, 1929

Thunder in the black skies beating down the rain,
Thunder in the black cliffs, looming o'er the main,
Thunder on the black sea and thunder in my brain.

God's on the night wind, Satan's on his throne
By the red lake lurid and great grim stone —
Still through the roofs of Hell the brooding thunders drone.

Trident for a rapier, Satan thrusts and foins
Crouching on his throne with his great goat loins —
Souls are his footstools and hearts are his coins.

Slave of all the ages, though lord of the air;
Solomon o'ercame him, set him roaring there,
Crouching on the coals where the great flames flare.

Thunder from the grim gulfs, out of cosmic deep
Where the red eyes glimmer and the black wings sweep,
Thunder down to Satan, wake him from his sleep!

Thunder on the shores of Hell, scattering the coal,
Riding down the mountain on the moon-mare's foal,
Blasting out the caves of the gnome and the troll.

Satan, brother Satan, rise and break your chain!
Solomon is dust and his spells grow vain —
Rise through the world in the thunder and the rain.

Rush upon the cities, roaring in your might,
Break down the towers in the moon's pale light,
Build a wall of corpses for God's great sight,
Quench the red thunder in my brain this night.